"I Guess I Should Thank You For Saving My Honor."

"You make me sound like some kind of white knight or something. A knight," Troy repeated, then snorted a disbelieving laugh. He nestled his cheek against Shelby's neck, then laid his head back down on the pillow.

He *was* a knight, she reflected wistfully, listening as his heavy breathing grew rhythmic. Troy had saved her family from the disgrace associated with having an unwed pregnant daughter, and he'd saved her child from the stigma of being born out of wedlock. Yes, he was a white knight, all right.

But could she keep this cowboy knight in her little Texas castle…forever?

Dear Reader,

Silhouette is celebrating our 20th anniversary in 2000, and the latest powerful, passionate, provocative love stories from Silhouette Desire are as hot as that steamy summer weather!

For August's MAN OF THE MONTH, the fabulous BJ James begins her brand-new miniseries, MEN OF BELLE TERRE. In *The Return of Adams Cade*, a self-made millionaire returns home to find redemption in the arms of his first love.

Beloved author Cait London delivers another knockout in THE TALLCHIEFS miniseries with *Tallchief: The Homecoming,* also part of the highly sensual Desire promotion BODY & SOUL. And Desire is proud to present *Bride of Fortune* by Leanne Banks, the launch title of FORTUNE'S CHILDREN: THE GROOMS, another exciting spin-off of the bestselling Silhouette FORTUNE'S CHILDREN continuity miniseries.

BACHELOR BATTALION marches on with Maureen Child's *The Last Santini Virgin,* in which a military man's passion for a feisty virgin weakens his resolve not to marry. *In Name Only* is how a sexy rodeo cowboy agrees to temporarily wed a pregnant preacher's daughter in the second book of Peggy Moreland's miniseries TEXAS GROOMS. And Christy Lockhart reconciles a once-married couple who are stranded together in a wintry cabin during *One Snowbound Weekend....*

So indulge yourself by purchasing all six of these summer delights from Silhouette Desire...and read them in air-conditioned comfort.

Enjoy!

Joan Marlow Golan

Joan Marlow Golan
Senior Editor, Silhouette Desire

Please address questions and book requests to:
Silhouette Reader Service
U.S.: 3010 Walden Ave., P.O. Box 1325, Buffalo, NY 14269
Canadian: P.O. Box 609, Fort Erie, Ont. L2A 5X3

In Name Only
PEGGY MORELAND

Silhouette® Desire®

Published by Silhouette Books

America's Publisher of Contemporary Romance

Special thanks to Merry Stahel for sharing with me special memories of her own Las Vegas wedding. Thanks, Merry!

And to Dr. Bruce Tagge, for answering questions pertaining to pregnancy complications. Thanks, Bruce!

SILHOUETTE BOOKS

ISBN 0-373-76313-1

IN NAME ONLY

Copyright © 2000 by Peggy Bozeman Morse

This edition published by arrangement with Harlequin Books S.A.

® and TM are trademarks of Harlequin Books S.A., used under license. Trademarks indicated with ® are registered in the United States Patent and Trademark Office, the Canadian Trade Marks Office and in other countries.

Visit Silhouette at www.eHarlequin.com

Printed in U.S.A.

PEGGY MORELAND

published her first romance with Silhouette in 1989 and continues to delight readers with stories set in her home state of Texas. Winner of the National Readers' Choice Award, a nominee for the *Romantic Times Magazine* Reviewer's Choice Award and a finalist for the prestigious RITA Award, Peggy has appeared on the *USA Today* and Waldenbooks bestseller lists. When not writing, she enjoys spending time at the farm riding her quarter horse, Lo-Jump. She, her husband and three children make their home in Round Rock, Texas. You may write to Peggy at P.O. Box 2453, Round Rock, TX 78680-2453.

IT'S OUR 20th ANNIVERSARY!
We'll be celebrating all year,
Continuing with these fabulous titles,
On sale in August 2000.

One

A black cat streaked in front of the diner's entrance and directly across Troy Jacobs's path. Startled, Troy stumbled to a stop, then frowned as he watched the cat dart around the side of the building and disappear from sight. Well aware of the superstitions associated with black cats, he knew he should probably turn right around and head in the opposite direction.

But he didn't.

He figured a black cat crossing his path couldn't hurt his current run of luck. It was already running so low on the downside of bad he didn't think it could possibly get any worse.

With a rueful shake of his head, he pushed open the door, stepped inside and bumped into the Corley brothers who were just leaving.

He nodded a greeting to the cowboys as he pulled off his hat.

Rudy, the older of the two, clapped a hand on Troy's shoulder. "Too bad about that steer you drew tonight. I've never seen one drop and cut behind a hazer as fast as that one. Didn't even give you a fair chance to throw him."

Troy nodded his agreement. "Yeah, well, seems as if I'm drawing all the strange ones lately."

Rudy wagged his head sympathetically, then grinned and gave Troy a friendly punch on the arm. "But, hey, your luck's bound to change soon, right? This losing streak can't last forever."

Troy tried to force a game smile—though he certainly didn't feel the sentiment—but he couldn't seem to muster the enthusiasm required for the action. After putting up entry fees for three months without any wins to offset his expenses, it was hard to find anything to smile about. "I sure hope so," he said with a resigned sigh, "because if it doesn't, I might have to break down and sell my horse."

Rudy hooted a laugh and slapped Troy on the back. "If it comes to that, you give me a call. I've always admired Danny Boy. There's not a horse around with more heart." Rudy snugged his cowboy hat over his head and reached for the door, touching a finger to the hat's brim in farewell. "See you around, Troy."

"Yeah," Troy replied with a jerk of his chin. "See you."

Road noise from the highway that stretched in front of the truck stop rushed in as the Corley brothers left, then dulled to a low roar when the door closed behind the two men.

Wishing he'd arrived earlier so that he could've shared a meal with the two cowboys and avoided eating alone, Troy looked around the nearly empty room, searching for a hostess. He didn't see one, but at this hour of the night, he wasn't surprised. The only customers remaining were a couple of truck drivers huddled at the counter, nursing thick porcelain mugs of steaming coffee, and a woman who sat alone in a booth on the opposite side of the room. When Troy glanced the woman's way, he found her staring at him, but she quickly looked away when their gazes met, a blush staining her cheeks.

She was a pretty little thing, he noted absently. Blond, with big blue eyes, a peaches-and-cream complexion…and from what he could see, a nice figure. If Pete was with him, Troy knew his friend would already be hustling over to her table and striking up a conversation. Pete did love women. And women seemed to love Pete.

He smiled inwardly as he thought of his friend, wondering if he ought to mosey over and try one of Pete's tactics on the woman and see if she'd be willing to share her table with him…but he quickly discarded the notion. He wasn't like Pete who could charm the skin off a snake and the clothes off a woman's back, and he'd rather suffer the agony of eating alone than take a chance on being rejected.

Instead, he plucked a menu from the rack on the wall and dropped down in a booth near the front door, placing his cowboy hat crown side up on the seat beside him.

He flipped open the menu and studied it, wishing Pete and Clayton, his traveling buddies, were with him. He hated like hell eating alone. But Pete was still at Clayton's ranch, keeping an eye on things, while Clayton chased after his wife in hopes of talking her out of leaving him. Personally, he hoped Clayton was successful. He liked Rena, though he wondered sometimes why she'd put up with Clayton's indifference for so long.

"What can I get you, cowboy?"

Troy looked up and found a waitress standing beside the booth, the stubbed point of her pencil poised over a pad. He offered her an easy smile. "What would you recommend?"

She tucked the pencil behind her ear and shifted her

weight, lifting a foot to rub it along the back of a calf that
he was sure was aching after a long day waiting tables.
"Meat loaf's fresh and it comes with a side of green beans,
mashed potatoes and a square of cornbread. Six-fifty, or
seven dollars if you order a drink."

Troy closed his menu and handed it to her. "Sounds
good to me. And I'd like a cup of coffee, when you have
the time."

"Sure thing." Dropping the pad into her apron pocket,
she headed for the counter.

Troy turned his face toward the window and stared out
at the highway, watching the occasional eighteen-wheeler
roar by. Superimposed on the glass was a reflection of the
café's interior. In it he saw the waitress snag a pot of coffee
from the warming plate and head back his way. Turning,
he reared back to give her room as she upended a porcelain
mug.

"Did you compete in the rodeo tonight?" she asked as
she filled his cup.

"Yes, ma'am, I did."

Straightening, she rested the pot of coffee on the edge
of the table and looked at him suspiciously. "You a bull
rider?"

Troy chuckled and shook his head. "No, ma'am. There's
not enough money in the world to persuade me to climb
on the back of some rank bull."

She returned his smile, revealing a gold-capped front
tooth. "I didn't think so. The bull riders who pass through
here are a cocky bunch. And they sure as heck don't have
your manners," she added wryly.

Troy tossed back his head and laughed. "You can thank
my grandmother for the manners. She pounded them into
me from an early age."

She shifted her weight from one crepe-soled shoe to the
other. "If you're not a bull rider, then what are you?"

"A steer wrestler."

She arched a brow. "Really? I'd think steer wrestling would be as dangerous as bull riding."

With the long stretch of loneliness that awaited him on the drive ahead, Troy was glad for the company. Settling in for a visit, he wrapped his hands around the mug, absorbing its warmth, and lifted a shoulder. "Not to my way of thinking. If a man's got a good horse and a good hazer, he narrows the odds some in his favor."

A shiver shook her thin shoulders beneath a uniform about a size too big for her bony frame. "I can't imagine jumping off a running horse and wrestling a horned steer to the ground. I'd be afraid one of those horns would run straight through me."

Troy chuckled. "It happens, now and again, but not as often as a bull turning on a rider he's thrown and goring him."

When a bell pinged impatiently, the waitress glanced over her shoulder and saw the truck drivers waiting beside the cash register. She offered Troy an apologetic smile as she tipped her head toward the counter. "Duty calls. I'll get your order out to you quick as I can."

"No hurry, ma'am."

She winked and gave his hand a motherly pat. "The next time you see your grandmother you tell her she did a fine job raising you."

Troy watched the waitress hustle over to the cash register, sobered by the reminder of his grandmother. Then, with a sigh, he turned his gaze back to the window. Yeah, he'd tell Granny all right, he thought sadly. But he doubted his grandmother would even recognize him, much less understand the compliment enough to appreciate it. Alzheimer's had stolen a mind that had remained sharp for more than seventy years, and overnight had turned his grandmother into a stranger to him. He always came away from the nursing home where she now lived, wondering how life could be so cruel to a woman with a heart as big as hers. She'd worked hard all her life, and when she should've been enjoying her golden years, she'd taken in Troy to raise after his mother had died.

He caught a movement on the window's reflection and saw that the waitress was heading back his way, juggling his dinner. Shaking off the melancholy thoughts of his grandmother, he leaned back and forced a grateful smile for the waitress as she slid the plate and basket of cornbread in front of him. "Thanks."

"Can I get you anything else?"

He glanced at the generous helpings on the plate. "No, ma'am. This'll be fine for now."

As she went back to her duties, Troy unwrapped his silverware, shook out his napkin and spread it over his thigh. His mouth watering at the tempting scents that rose to meet his nose, he lifted the fork and dug in.

He'd cleaned about half his plate when he felt the hair on the back of his neck prickle. He glanced over and caught the woman in the booth on the opposite side of the room staring at him again. Her expression was an odd mixture of appraisal and desperation, which he found a bit unnerving. But damn she was a pretty little thing. All soft and feminine and innocent, much like the angels he remembered pictured in the family Bible his grandmother kept on the coffee table in the front room of the home they'd once shared.

Baffled by the intensity with which she was studying him, he dabbed the napkin at the corner of his mouth, wondering if he had food on his face or something. He nodded a quick, embarrassed greeting, then turned his attention back to his meal.

He hadn't taken more than two bites when a shadow fell across his plate. He looked up and found the woman standing beside his booth. She was even prettier up close, but she had a scared-rabbit look about her that concerned him.

"I apologize for interrupting your dinner," she said, her fingers clutched tightly around the strap of a shoulder purse, "but would you mind if I join you for a minute?"

Her voice was as sweet as her face, but there was a quaver in it that confirmed his suspicion that something was bothering her.

He rose and gestured to the bench opposite him. "No, ma'am, I sure don't. In fact, I'd welcome the company."

She slipped into the booth and waited for him to take his seat again. Once he had, she stretched a hand across the table. "I'm Shelby Cannon."

He wiped his palm down his thigh before taking her hand in his. Small. Delicately boned. His own work-roughened hand swallowed her smaller one. "Troy Jacobs," he returned. "It's a pleasure to meet you, ma'am."

Her eyes sharpened when his fingers closed around hers, and he couldn't help wondering if she felt the same kick to the system as he had when their palms first met.

Slowly she withdrew her hand, then fisted it with the other on her lap. "Mr. Jacobs—"

"Troy," he insisted, and smiled, hoping to put her at ease.

She inhaled deeply. "Troy, then," she said, and forced a polite, if tremulous, smile in return. "I know this may seem presumptuous of me to approach you in this way, but I'm running short of time and forced to be blunt." She drew in another deep breath, then leaned toward him, leveling her gaze on his. "Are you married?"

The question came out of left field, catching him totally off guard. He wondered if she was planning on trying to pick him up, though she certainly didn't look the type. "No ma'am," he replied cautiously.

Her shoulders sagged in relief. "Thank goodness. I didn't see a ring, but I had to make certain."

"Are you?" he asked, thinking he ought to establish her marital status, since she'd considered his so important.

She shook her head, then leaned closer. "I didn't mean to eavesdrop, but I couldn't help overhearing your conversation, earlier, when you were talking to those two men who were leaving."

"The Corley brothers?" At her nod, he chuckled. "Yes, ma'am. Me and the Corleys go way back. They're steer wrestlers, too, and we've competed against each other over the years. Lately, though, they've been collecting all the winnings."

She closed her hands around the edge of the scarred table and drew herself forward, her expression growing more earnest. "I heard you say that you might have to sell your horse if your luck didn't change pretty soon."

His ego took a beating, knowing that she'd overheard that. Not that he was desperate for money. He wasn't. The comment had been made in jest. What embarrassed him was that she was aware of his current losing streak. He dropped his gaze and stirred his fork through his mashed potatoes. "My situation's not quite as bad as it sounds."

"How much is your horse worth?"

He jerked up his head to peer at her. "You're wanting to buy my horse?"

Obviously startled by the question, she shook her head. "Oh, no! I don't want to *buy* your horse. Heavens!" She laughed weakly and placed a hand over her breasts, as if the idea alone was enough to bring on a heart attack. "I wouldn't know what to do with a horse. I've never even been on one."

"So why do you want to know how much he's worth?"

"I…I—" She pressed her lips together and forced her chin up a notch. "I'm just interested, is all."

"Twenty-five thousand."

Her mouth dropped open. "Twenty-five thousand dollars!" At Troy's nod, she sank weakly against the back of the booth. "Twenty-five thousand dollars," she repeated, then closed her eyes, her shoulders sagging in defeat.

When she opened her eyes, Troy would have sworn he saw tears in them.

"I don't have that much money," she said, her voice heavy with regret. She pushed to her feet. "Thank you for your time, Troy. I'm sorry to have bothered you."

He stretched a hand across the table, stopping her. "Hold on a minute." She glanced at the hand that gripped her arm, then back at him and slowly sank back down, her gaze now watchful. Realizing he'd frightened her, Troy released his hold on her. "I thought you said you wanted to buy my horse?"

"Oh, no! I just wanted to know how much he was worth."

"Why?"

She shifted uneasily on the booth. "Well," she began, then averted her gaze, her cheeks turning pink again. "I was hoping that I could...well, that I could make a trade with you."

"If you don't want my horse, then what is it you want me to trade?"

He watched the pink turn a brilliant red. She plucked a paper napkin from the holder on the table and kept her gaze on her fingers as she began to shred it.

"Your name," she said in a low voice.

Troy leaned closer, sure that he'd misunderstood her. "My name?"

A tear rolled over her lower lashes and down her cheek. She swiped at it furiously with the shredded napkin. "Yes. Your name." Another tear quickly fell to replace the first.

Troy lifted a hip and worked a handkerchief from his back pocket and offered it to her.

"Thank you," she murmured, sniffing as she blotted the handkerchief beneath her eyes.

"Why would you want my name?" he asked in confusion.

"Not just your name, actually." She caught her lower lip between her teeth.

Frustrated, Troy shoved aside his plate and leaned forward, resting his forearms on the table. "Maybe you should tell me just exactly what it is you want from me."

She pressed the handkerchief against her lips, then fanned it in front of her eyes when they filled with tears again. "I'm sorry. I don't mean to cry. It's just that I had so hoped you would agree to marry me and let me use your name."

Troy was sure that he had stepped into a scene from the Twilight Zone. "Did you say *marry* you?"

She pressed the handkerchief beneath her nose and nodded. "I'd pay you, of course," she hurried to explain. "I've got the money." She rolled her eyes toward the ceiling. "But not $25,000. I only have about $5,000 in my savings account."

Troy braced his hands against the edge of the table, pushed himself back against the seat and released a shuddering breath. He stared at her a long moment, trying to figure her angle. "And why would a pretty young lady like yourself want to marry an old cowboy like me? Hell," he said, gesturing at her. "You don't even know me."

Her eyes flew wide. "Oh, no! I don't want to marry you—I mean, at least, not in the sense you must think. I just need your name. My plan was for us to marry, go our separate ways, then divorce after the baby is born."

Troy choked, his eyes going wide. "Baby?" he gasped hoarsely.

Tears filled her eyes. "Yes…baby." She pressed her hand over her stomach, her lips trembling. "I'm pregnant."

He dropped his gaze to her hand and the flat stomach beneath it. The *Twilight Zone,* he told himself again, swallowing hard. He'd landed himself in an episode of the *Twilight Zone.* Or maybe he'd been set up for one of those television shows where they caught an unsuspecting person in an unbelievable situation and filmed his response for all of America to laugh at later. He glanced quickly around, looking for the hidden camera. But all he saw were empty booths and the waitress working at the counter, refilling salt and pepper shakers.

Slowly he brought his gaze back to Shelby's.

"Baby," he repeated dully.

She nodded.

"Why don't you just ask the man who fathered the child to marry you?"

Her shoulders hitched and she pressed the handkerchief over her mouth to stifle the sob that bubbled up. Then she looked up at him, her blue eyes filled with a heartbreaking mixture of pain and humiliation. "I…I did, but h-he refused."

Frustrated by the entire conversation, Troy didn't even try to hide the disgust in his voice. "You should've thought of the consequences before you slept with the guy. Or at least taken the necessary precautions. Pregnancy is easy enough to avoid these days."

Her chin came up at his accusatory tone, and her eyes turned a steely blue. She cut a glance toward the waitress to make certain his comment hadn't been overheard, then leaned across the table and narrowed her eyes. "I did," she whispered angrily. "But unfortunately not *all* precautionary measures are 100 percent fail-safe." She tossed his handkerchief on the table. "Oh, just forget it," she snapped as she scooted from the booth. "I thought this might be the perfect solution to both our problems, but I can see that I was wrong." Stalking to the door, she pushed her way furiously to the outside, sending the cowbell hanging over the door clanking loudly.

Frowning, Troy watched her through the window as she marched across the parking lot, her shoulders square, her head high. Not your problem, Jacobs, he told himself as he watched her jerk open her car door and slip inside. The vehicle rocked hard when she slammed the door behind her. Not your problem, he told himself again when—to his surprise—she wrapped her arms around the steering wheel and buried her face against it. He watched the sobs wrack her slim shoulders…and a fist closed around his heart and squeezed.

His name. All the lady wanted was his name, for God's sake. Was that so much to ask? It wasn't as if she had asked him to donate a kidney, or something. And it was only for a couple of months, just long enough to give her baby a name and save it the shame of being labeled a bastard. And who could understand better than Troy Jacobs the stigma attached to being born out of wedlock? Maybe his own life would have been a bit different if his mother had done what this woman was trying to do.

"Damn," he swore under his breath. He grabbed his hat and rammed it on his head and pushed himself from the booth. Digging his wallet from his back pocket, he pulled out a twenty and tossed it on the table. "Much obliged," he called to the waitress and waved to her as he pushed through the door.

When he reached Shelby's car, he grabbed the door handle and swore again when he discovered it was locked. He slammed a fist against the window. "Open up," he ordered angrily.

She turned her tear-streaked face to glare up at him. "Go

away," she sobbed, and buried her face against her hands
again.

Troy pounded his fist on the glass. "Either you open the
door or I'm busting out the glass. Your choice."

Her face twisted with fury, she sat up and rolled down
the window. "Say what you have to say, then leave," she
ordered tersely. "This isn't your problem."

Scowling, he reached inside and unlocked the door himself. "I don't think you want what I have to say broadcast
all over the parking lot." He bumped his hip against her
side, forcing her to scoot over. "And no, it's not my problem," he said as he sat down on the seat still warm from
her bottom. He felt around for the release and shoved the
seat back, giving him room to stretch out his long legs. He
slammed the door with the same degree of frustration as
she had, then twisted around on the seat to face her. The
fact that she shrank away from him, didn't go unnoticed.
It even shamed him a bit to see a woman cower from him.
"How much?"

Startled, she stammered, "W-what?"

"How much?" he repeated angrily. "How much are you
willing to pay me for my name?"

Slowly she sat up straighter, her gaze fixed on his face.
"Five thousand dollars."

"And how long do we have to stay married?"

"Until the baby's born."

"When's it due?"

"The fifth of March. I'm three months along."

Amazed, he glanced down at her stomach where she'd
unconsciously pressed a hand, then slowly lifted his gaze
to hers again. "But you're not even showing."

She dipped her chin and smoothed a hand across her
abdomen. "No. Thankfully. But I will be before long."

Setting his jaw, he frowned at her. "What would be expected of me?"

"Nothing," she assured him quickly, then caught her lip between her teeth as if catching herself in a lie. "Well, I do need you to do one thing."

"What?"

"Go home with me and meet my parents. Otherwise," she hurried to explain, "they might not believe I'm really married."

Troy groaned and slumped down in the seat. "I have to meet your parents?" He rolled his head to the side to look at her. "Couldn't you just show them the marriage license?"

She clamped her lips together, frowning. "No, I can't just show them the marriage license," she mimicked sarcastically. "My father is going to be angry enough that we didn't marry in the church. He is the pastor, after all, and—"

Troy snapped up his head. "The pastor!" he shouted. "Your daddy is a preacher?"

She gulped and shrank away from him, nodding.

Troy dropped his head back and groaned. "A preacher," he repeated miserably. "Pete and Clayton are never going to believe this. Hell, I'm not even sure I believe it myself!" Sighing, he turned his face to the side window and stared out at the darkness beyond. From the far side of the parking lot, a pair of green eyes peered back at him.

The black cat.

Maybe I should've turned around and headed the other way, he thought miserably.

But it was too late now. Seemed he'd just agreed to sell his name to a pregnant preacher's daughter to the tune of five thousand dollars.

Two

Though it was almost dawn and the sky still clung to the colors of midnight, the street Troy drove his truck down was bright as midday.

Las Vegas.

He gave his head a shake, then angled it a bit to steal a glance at the woman who slept in the passenger seat beside him. She sat with her head tipped against the window, her bare feet tucked up underneath her and hidden by her full, broomstick skirt. She looked so innocent in sleep, like an angel, even more so than when she was awake, which was pretty darn angelic in Troy's estimation. Something told him, though, that this little angel's preacher-daddy wasn't going to think too highly of a Las Vegas wedding for his daughter.

With another shake of his head, he turned his face to the windshield again and the street beyond. "Shelby?" he called softly, not wanting to startle her.

She shifted, snuggling a hand beneath her cheek, and a bare toe slipped from beneath the folds of her skirt, its nail painted a soft, shell-pink. As he watched, the toe curled as if inviting his touch.

Finding the sight oddly arousing—and himself more than a little tempted to accept the invitation and stroke a hand along that foot and up the smooth, bare leg beneath the skirt—he set his jaw and forced his gaze away. Clearing his throat, he tried not to think about that bare toe, or the stretch of leg attached to it, and attempted again to rouse her. "Shelby?"

"Hmmm?" she hummed sleepily.

"Better wake up. We're here."

Instantly alert, she straightened, slowly unwinding her legs and slipping her feet gracefully to the floor. Brushing her hair back from her face, she leaned forward to peer through the windshield. Her eyes grew wide at the sight that greeted her.

"Oh, my stars," she murmured, darting her eyes from one side of the street to the other, where elaborately designed hotels and brightly lit casinos seemed to mushroom from the very edge of the sidewalk and shoot straight up to the sky. A billboard at the intersection they approached pictured a woman on a swing inside a gilded cage, wearing nothing but feathers and spangles.

"Did you see that?" she whispered on a long, disbelieving breath. As they passed through the intersection, she twisted her head around, keeping her gaze riveted on the scantily clad woman pictured on the massive billboard.

"Ever been to Las Vegas before?" Troy asked, unable to suppress the smile her shocked expression drew.

"No," she said and turned to look at him, her eyes wide, her cheeks flushed.

"Welcome to the den of iniquity," he said, waving an expansive hand at the view before them.

She sank back against the seat and swallowed hard, staring. "Is it always like this?" she murmured.

"Like what?"

"So...so full of life," she said, gesturing helplessly to the people who crowded the sidewalks.

"Yep. Nobody sleeps in Las Vegas. It's one of the unwritten rules." Realizing that he had no idea where he was headed, Troy steered the truck onto a side street beside a hotel's entrance and stopped.

She peered through the window at the hotel's revolving door, then turned slowly to look at him. "Why are you stopping here?"

He saw the suspicion in her eyes, heard it in her voice, and snorted, pulling on the emergency brake before killing the engine. "'Cause I don't know where we're going, that's why," he reminded her. "Do you?"

She turned to peer through the window again at the hotel beyond. "No," she said, her nervousness obvious. "But I'd think we'd need to find a chapel or something, wouldn't we? Not a hotel."

"That'd be my guess." He braced a hand against the steering wheel, inhaled deeply, then slowly released it, questioning again his sanity in allowing himself to be suckered into this crazy scheme of hers. "Are you sure you want to go through with this?"

She snapped her head around to peer at him, her eyes wider than before. "Yes! I have to."

"You don't *have* to," he reminded her. "You could always just tell your parents about the baby. They might be more understanding than you think."

"Oh, no," she said, frantically shaking her head. "My father would never understand." She gulped, swallowed, then turned to stare at the windshield, though he was sure she saw nothing on the glass but an image of her father's irate face. "Never," she repeated in a hoarse whisper.

Troy sighed. "What about a friend, then? Surely there's someone you know who would agree to marry you?"

"No," she said, and shook her head again. "No one. Dunning is a small town. Everybody knows everybody." She lifted a shoulder. "And even if I did ask someone, everyone in town, my father included, would know the real reason for the marriage before the ink was dry on the marriage certificate. I won't subject my family to that embarrassment."

Sighing, Troy pushed open his door, but his foot had barely touched the ground before Shelby was diving across the console and grabbing his arm, stopping him.

"Where are you going?" she cried, her eyes wide with alarm.

He eased his arm from the death grip with which she held him. "I'm just going to step into that hotel there," he said, nodding toward it, "and see if they have some brochures on wedding chapels in the area. I'll be right back."

Sinking back onto her seat, she slowly nodded. "Good idea," she murmured, then caught her lower lip between her teeth and turned her face toward the passenger window. A woman strolled past, wearing three-inch-spike heels, her hips swaying suggestively beneath a skintight gold lamé miniskirt, her breasts overflowing the top of a leopard print bustier. The woman glanced Shelby's way, puckered her heavily painted lips and blew a kiss.

Shelby gasped and whirled to look at Troy. "Did you see that?" she cried in a shocked whisper. "That woman was a *man!*"

"Transvestite," Troy corrected, trying not to laugh. "You'll see a lot of them around here."

Shelby whipped her head back around to the window just as a man staggered by, obviously drunk. He fell against the hood of the truck, cursed soundly, then straightened and staggered on. Shelby gulped, then swallowed as she lifted a discreet hand to depress the door lock. "Maybe you better hurry, okay?" she whispered to Troy.

He planned to do just that, but hadn't made it more than halfway up the hotel's inclined drive when he heard the truck door slam. He glanced behind him and saw Shelby hurrying toward him, her shoulder bag hugged tight at her side.

"I thought I might just as well go with you," she murmured, glancing nervously around. "Might save us a little time."

Shaking his head, Troy took her by the elbow and guided her up the walk. An angel's first visit to Sodom and Gomorrah, he thought wryly. He wondered if she'd get soot on her wings.

Stepping back, he allowed Shelby to enter the revolving door first, then slipped into the compartment behind her, following as she stepped out, gaping into the ornately decorated hotel. Seeing the concierge's desk, he caught her elbow and quickly ushered her toward the rack of brochures displayed beside it. While she waited behind him, he thumbed through the brochures, selecting several that advertised wedding chapels.

"How about this one?" he asked, holding up a brochure over his shoulder for her approval. When she didn't respond, he turned, and his heart skipped a beat when he found she wasn't standing behind him. Sure that he'd lost her—or worse, someone had kidnapped her—he started walking, casting his gaze left and right, searching for her.

He found her not more than thirty feet away, standing in front of a slot machine, her eyes round in wonder as she stared at the machine's flashing lights.

"Damn, Shelby," he complained. "I thought I'd lost you."

She jumped, startled, then turned to look guiltily up at

him. "I'm sorry. But I've never seen a slot machine before and wanted to see how one works."

Unable to believe that anyone was *that* innocent, he dug a hand in his pocket and pulled out a quarter. "Here. Give it a try."

She hesitated a second, biting her lower lip, then took the quarter from him and sat down in front of the machine. "What do I do?" she asked uncertainly, placing her purse primly on pressed-together knees.

"Just slip the quarter in that slot there," he said, pointing, "then push the spin button. Or, if you want to do it the old-fashioned way, you can pull down the arm at the side of the machine."

He bit back a grin when he saw the way her fingers trembled as she dropped the coin into the slot. Bracing his hands on his thighs, he leaned forward as she pulled down the arm, putting his face on the same level with hers, then watched with her as the images flashed by. When the wheel stopped, three cherries were displayed. Immediately lights started flashing, the national anthem blared from a hidden speaker within the machine…and Troy gaped.

She jumped up from the stool, nearly knocking him down. "Did I do something wrong?" she asked, pressing herself against his side, trembling, as she stared in horror at the machine.

"Wrong?" Chuckling, Troy leaned over and punched the cash out button, and tokens clinked musically as they began to spill into the payoff return. "I'd say you definitely did something right. You hit the jackpot."

"Jackpot?" she repeated, staring at him. Then her mouth dropped open and she let out a squeal that had more than a few heads turning their way. Before he had a chance to brace himself, she threw herself into his arms. "Oh, Troy! That's marvelous! You won! You won!"

For a moment Troy could do nothing but hold on to her

as she jumped up and down in his arms, painfully aware of the swell of her breasts chafing against his chest, the slender arms wrapped around his neck, her womanly scent. But then what she'd said slowly registered.

He'd won?

Before he could argue the point, she was whirling away and dropping to her knees to pick up coins from the floor as they spilled from the brimming payoff return. "Oh, my heavens, Troy!" she exclaimed, her eyes shining brighter than any star he'd ever seen light a night sky. "There must be hundreds of dollars here. Maybe thousands! You're rich!"

"Me!" he said in dismay, staring at her as she scrambled around on the floor, retrieving dropped tokens. "Hell, that money's not mine."

She stopped suddenly and glanced up, looking like a kid who'd dropped her ice cream cone before she'd gotten the first lick. "It's not?"

"Hell, no! That money's yours! You were the one behind the controls."

"Oh, no," she said, and dropped the tokens back into the bin, then dusted her hands, as if to deny ownership. "It's yours. It was *your* quarter that I inserted into the machine. Not mine."

Troy stared at her a long moment, unable to believe what he was hearing. Any other woman would probably already be at the cashier's box, cashing in the tokens and thinking about a zillion ways to spend the money, not arguing over ownership. Shaking his head, he pulled off his cowboy hat. "An angel," he muttered under his breath as he stooped to scrape the mountain of tokens into the crown of his hat. And a lucky angel, at that.

As he straightened, having to use both hands to support the loaded hat, he glanced toward the crap tables, wondering if Shelby might like to try her hand at that game of chance. Lady Luck definitely seemed to be riding on her shoulder that night. But then he glanced back at her and saw her standing with her purse hugged at her side, peering at the entrance, that worried look in her eyes again.

Sighing, he jerked his chin in the direction of the cashier's booth. "Let's cash this in and get out of here," he said gruffly. "We can fight over who gets stuck with the winnings later."

"No," Shelby said, frowning slightly as she studied the tiny chapel tucked against the side of the hotel. Red neon lights flashed on and off beneath an oversize set of plaster wedding bells draped with satin-like ribbon painted a garish silver. The blinking sign promised a drive-through wedding ceremony for under twenty-five dollars. "This one is just too…too…"

"Tacky?" Troy offered helpfully.

"Yes," she replied, her shoulders sagging in defeat. "Much too tacky."

It was the fourth chapel Troy had driven by and the fourth Shelby had eliminated, for one reason or another. Personally, he thought the Elvis wedding might have been kind of fun, definitely something to tell the guys about later, but she had nixed that one with barely a glance.

Wearily he plucked another brochure from the pile littering the console. "How about this one?" he asked, holding the brochure out for her inspection. "The Little Church of the West. The name has a nice ring to it, plus it actually looks like a real church. See?"

Shelby studied the photo he indicated and the creases on her forehead slowly smoothed. "That's it," she said, then tipped her face up to Troy's, her smile radiant. "That's the one."

"You sure?" he asked uncertainly.

"Positive," she said, and took the brochure from his

hand. "And it isn't too far," she added, studying the map. She lifted a hand and pointed a finger. "Three blocks ahead, near the end of the strip. The chapel should be right there."

Troy stood back while Shelby talked to the receptionist, his cowboy hat clasped between his wide hands, feeling much like what he thought a corpse might feel—if they could feel anything—while waiting for their casket to be selected.

"And which package would you like?" the receptionist asked, turning a colorfully printed brochure around on the desk for Shelby's inspection. "A custom package? Or perhaps our luxury package?"

"Oh, I don't know," Shelby replied uncertainly, and turned to give Troy a helpless look. He arched a brow and lifted a shoulder, letting her know the decision was hers to make. "Just the basic one, I guess," she said, turning back to the woman.

"We offer several services and items for our guests' convenience. Surely you'd like to have a video recording of your ceremony to share with your family back home?"

"Oh, no," Shelby said with a quick shake of her head. "That won't be necessary."

"How about photographs, then? We have a professional photographer on hand who takes wonderful pictures. I'm sure you'll want a set to commemorate the event."

"No," Shelby said slowly, and Troy thought he heard tears in her voice. "I...I don't think so."

"Flowers?" the receptionist offered, peeking around Shelby to peer at Troy, her arched eyebrows indicating that she considered him to be the ultimate tightwad.

"N-no. Just—"

Troy saw Shelby's chin begin to quiver and knew he hadn't been mistaken. She was definitely about to turn on the waterworks, which didn't surprise him. He was amazed she'd made it this far without falling apart. A woman like her had probably dreamed for years about her wedding day…and, more than likely, those dreams had never included a late-night drive to Las Vegas in a one-ton dually with some old cowboy she'd picked up at a truck stop.

And the receptionist wasn't helping things a bit with her unending questions and suggestions. Though he realized that the woman had no clue about the circumstances behind this trumped-up marriage, he'd like nothing better than to wring her pretty neck for reminding Shelby of what all a wedding ceremony *should* consist of.

Feeling the need to intercede and spare Shelby any more anguish, he slipped between her and the receptionist and caught Shelby by the elbows, gently squeezing and forcing her gaze to his. "Why don't you wait out in the truck?" he suggested quietly. "I'll take care of the arrangements."

Shelby nodded tearfully and turned away, pressing her fingers against her lips.

Troy waited until the door closed behind her, then dropped his hat on the desk and planted his wide hands on either side of it. He scowled down at the woman opposite him.

"We just want to get married, okay?" he said, struggling to remain calm. "Just the basics. A preacher, a little organ music and a witness to sign the certificate once we're done. Think you can handle that?"

"Well, of course," the woman replied in surprise. "We can provide any type of ceremony you wish."

He straightened, dragging his hat from the desk and clamped it down over his head. "Good. 'Cause that lady waiting out in the truck is going to have a baby in a few months, and I'd like to think we can pull this wedding off before the kid hits the ground."

The woman's jaw dropped open, then closed with a click.

She tore her gaze from his and opened a book. "W-we have an opening at ten this morning," she stammered, obviously flustered. "Would that fit in with your schedule?"

Troy flexed his shoulders, trying to ease the tension there. "Yeah. That'd be just dandy." He turned for the door, then stopped, paused a second, then glanced back. "And fix up a bouquet, would you? One with yellow rose buds. And throw in the cost of the photographer, too. Nothing fancy. Just a couple of shots."

Whether Shelby considered herself a real bride, or not, Troy told himself as he pushed his way through the door, she deserved flowers, even if her wedding was nothing but a sham. And he would need the pictures as proof this wedding had taken place, because he had a feeling that without them his buddies, Pete and Clayton, would never believe him when he told them he'd taken a detour off the rodeo circuit to marry a pregnant preacher's daughter in Las Vegas.

The line at the courthouse was longer than Troy had expected, and it took almost two hours for him and Shelby to acquire the paperwork required for a marriage in the state of Nevada.

Though he was sure his bride-to-be needed some time to compose herself before she was forced to lie, by pledging to love and honor a complete stranger for the rest of her life, Troy didn't have it to give her. As it was, they arrived back at the chapel with only seconds to spare.

The ceremony itself was pretty much a blur to Troy. He remembered standing at the altar, waiting while Shelby walked down the aisle, her steps slow and careful, in perfect rhythm with the traditional wedding march played by the organist he'd requested. He remembered seeing her white-knuckled fingers clasped around the bouquet of tiny yellow rose buds, and the shiny satin ribbons that had cascaded from it brushing against her knees with each slow step. He remembered her turning, once she'd reached the altar, and looking up at him.

But it was at that point that his memory failed. When she'd lifted those wide blue eyes up to his, eyes that glistened with unshed tears, eyes filled with so much innocence, so much trust…well, the sight had rendered him speechless. He was sure he must have repeated the vows the preacher had fed to him, but he didn't remember saying them, or even what they were. All he could remember were Shelby's eyes.

And something told him that those eyes, and the woman who possessed them, would haunt him for the rest of his life.

Troy pulled his truck into the alleyway, following the red taillights of Shelby's car. When she stopped, he did, too, then shut off the ignition and set the brake. Sighing wearily, he dragged a hand down his face before he opened the door and slid to the ground. He hadn't slept in over forty-eight hours, and the lack of rest was beginning to take its toll.

The long drive to Las Vegas. The return trip to Kingman, Arizona, where they'd retrieved Shelby's car from the truck stop where they'd met. The drive to Dunning, New Mexico, with her in the lead, guiding him back to her hometown. And few, very few, stops in between.

He glanced up, noticing the hesitancy with which she approached him. But he understood her sudden shyness. He felt rather awkward himself. Sort of like he had the time Pete had suckered him into taking a woman on a blind date. The drive to Dunning, each alone in their own vehicles, had stripped them of what bit of easiness they'd managed to develop during the trip to Las Vegas and back, and left them strangers again.

Not sure what the game plan was, now that they'd arrived in Dunning, he gestured toward the trailer. "I need to unload my horse and walk him around a bit, if that's okay."

Tucking her arms beneath her breasts, she nodded and stepped out of his way, then followed him to the rear of the trailer and watched silently as he unlocked the door and lowered the ramp.

"Danny Boy, isn't it?" she asked, obviously trying to make conversation as he backed the horse down the ramp.

"Yep. That's his name all right," he replied.

The horse spooked when his hooves hit the slick asphalt drive and skated a bit. Troy quickly tightened his grip on the lead rope. "Whoa, there, Danny Boy," he murmured softly, reaching to pat the horse's long neck. He glanced around as he soothed the animal, getting his bearings, then frowned. "Is this where you live?" he asked, turning his frown on Shelby.

She glanced over her shoulder at the block of dark, two-story buildings behind her. "Yes. I have an apartment over my shop." She looked at Troy again and shrugged self-consciously. "It's rather small, but it suits my needs."

He blew out a long breath, wondering how anybody could stand to live in such close quarters. For himself, he preferred open country with green pastures, rolling hills and a lake to fish, much like the land that surrounded his own home in East Texas.

"My parents live a couple of blocks away," she added. "In the parsonage beside the church."

At the reminder of her parents and the confrontation that awaited him in a few hours, Troy gave the lead rope a gentle tug. "Walk with me," he murmured, and caught Shelby's hand when she hesitated, pulling her along with him. He'd intended to release her hand once he had her in motion, but after feeling the tremble in her fingers, he found himself lacing his own fingers through hers and squeezing, knowing she was thinking about the confrontation with her parents, too. "They're going to be pretty disappointed, I'd guess," he offered quietly.

He saw her chin quiver before she caught herself and gave it a defiant lift.

"Yes, but they'll get over it."

He snorted a laugh. "That's yet to be seen." Having reached the end of the alley, he made a wide turn, then started back the way they'd come, stopping to let Danny Boy graze on a clump of grass growing at the edge of the dark drive. "I'll be leaving right after we tell them," he said after a moment. "I have a rodeo in Pecos on Friday."

He felt her fingers tense within his before she forced them to relax.

"That's fine," she replied, though he could tell the thought of being left alone to deal with her father scared the hell out of her. "I didn't expect you to stay."

"Exactly what am I supposed to say when we talk to them?"

"Nothing. I'll do the talking. I just need you there as proof."

"Proof," he repeated, then snorted again and shook his head. He released her hand and moved to tie Danny Boy to the side of the trailer. "I don't know what in the hell my being here proves."

"That I really do have a husband," she said in surprise, then clamped her lips together when he whipped his head around to look at her, one brow arched high. "Well, you know what I mean," she said, flustered.

Chuckling, Troy hung a net filled with hay within Danny Boy's reach, checked the level of water in the bucket, then placed a hand at the small of Shelby's back as he guided her to the narrow iron stairs that snaked up the rear of the building. "Yeah, I know what you mean."

He stepped out of the way while she dealt with the locks, then followed her into the dark apartment. He stopped, waiting for her to turn on some lights. When she did, he glanced around.

Though definitely larger than his horse trailer's sleeping loft, which was home to him when he was on the road, the room was small, yet comfortable. A love seat, upholstered in a floral chintz, dominated the center of the room. Two wicker chairs, one covered in a cheerful yellow fabric, the other in mint-green, sat opposite. Between the sofa and chairs was a small trunk that served as a coffee table of sorts, he supposed. As he studied the cozy seating arrangement, he tried to imagine squeezing his large frame onto that little sofa and shook his head.

"I told you it was small," she said as she headed for the kitchen tucked into a corner of the room. "Would you like something to drink?"

"No, thank you. Just a place to stretch out and catch some shut-eye."

She did a neat U-turn and lifted a hand to a panel of wood on the wall. Troy's chin nearly hit the floor when the panel lowered, exposing a bed.

"It's a Murphy bed," she said in explanation as she fluffed pillows. "I don't have a bedroom."

He snapped his head up to look at her. "You don't have a bedroom?"

Her cheeks pinkened, and she shook her head. "No. There's just this room and a bath." She settled the pillows at the head of the bed, then turned back the quilt, folding it neatly at the foot of the bed. "You can sleep here, and I'll sleep on the sofa."

Troy shifted his gaze to the sofa. It was so small he doubted even Shelby would be able to comfortably sleep on it. "I have a better idea," he said. "We'll share the bed. Me on top, you underneath." At the horrified look that came into her eyes, he felt his own cheeks heat. "The covers," he growled with an impatient wave of his hand at the bed. "I'll sleep on top of the covers, and you sleep underneath 'em."

Acutely aware of the man who lay on the bed beside her, Shelby held the sheet to her chin, her eyes wide as she stared at the dark ceiling. For the past forty-eight hours, ever since leaving Derrick's apartment after learning that he wanted nothing to do with her or their baby, she'd felt as if she was moving in a thick fog—lost, her thoughts jumbled, her nerves frayed—knowing that she couldn't go home and face her parents. Not without a husband, not without a name for the baby she carried.

She stole a glance at Troy who lay beside her, his eyes closed, his breathing even. She was still unable to believe that she'd had the nerve to ask a complete stranger to marry her. But even now, as she looked at him sleeping in her bed beside her, she didn't feel any fear. There was something about him—exactly what, she wasn't sure, but *something*—that told her he was a man whom she could trust.

She supposed it was fate that had placed them both at the truck stop's café at that exact moment in time. Her desperately in need of a husband to give her baby a name, and him in need of money so he wouldn't have to sell his horse. But whether it was fate or God's divining hand, she didn't think she would ever in a million years be able to repay him for the sacrifice he was making for her and her baby.

Even as the gratitude swelled inside her, guilt stabbed at her conscience as she realized she'd never properly thanked him.

"Troy?" she whispered urgently.

"Hmm?"

"Are you asleep?"

"No. But I'm working on it."

"Oh," she murmured in embarrassment, realizing too late how tired he must be. "Sorry. I didn't mean to disturb you."

"I wasn't asleep." He stretched his arms up to the ceiling and his bare feet over the foot of the bed, growling, then sighed, relaxing his body as he laced his fingers across his bare chest. "Whatcha need?"

"Nothing, really. I just wanted to—" she caught her bottom lip between her teeth, unable to find words adequate enough to convey the depth of her feelings "—to, well, to say thank you," she finished futilely. "I don't think I ever did."

"No thanks needed," he said gruffly.

"Oh, but there is," she insisted, turning her head to peer at him in the darkness. "You'll never know how much I appreciate your letting me use your name. *And* taking me to Las Vegas and handling all the arrangements," she added. "I hadn't thought about the time involved, obtaining a license and such. It was fortunate that you did."

"Like I said," he repeated. "No thanks needed. Now why don't you try to get some sleep?"

She turned her face back to the ceiling and pulled the sheet to her chin once more, but was too keyed up to even think about sleeping.

"Troy?" she whispered again.

"Hmm?"

"I don't think I can sleep."

He chuckled, the sound deep and throaty in the darkness. "Want me to tell you a bedtime story?"

"No," she replied, and bit back a smile at his teasing. "I think I'm a little old for that." She glanced over at him again and nervously pleated the sheet between her fingers. "But would you mind talking to me for a while?" she asked hopefully. "Just until I get sleepy?"

She could feel his gaze as he turned his head to peer at her, though his features were nothing but a play of shadows in the darkness. "About what?"

"Anything. Just talk. Tell me where you're from," she suggested and rolled to her side, slipping a hand beneath her pillow to support her head as she peered at him in the darkness.

He turned his face away to stare at the ceiling. "Texas. I've got a place near Tyler. Know where that is?"

"Yes," she said in surprise and pushed herself to an elbow. "I go to Canton for First Monday several times a year on buying trips. Tyler is near there, isn't it?"

"Not far. First Monday, huh?" She could hear the smile in his voice, though his face remained in shadows, hiding his expression. "Now there's a circus, if ever I've seen one."

She smiled, too, remembering her reaction upon visiting the flea market for the first time and experiencing its vastness and the variety of merchandise displayed there. "Yes, it is, and just as much fun."

"Haven't been in years," he replied absently, then added, "My place is about twenty or so miles from Canton."

"Really?" she said, her curiosity piqued as she dropped her head back to the pillow.

"My grandparents' place originally," he clarified. "About three hundred acres, give or take a few. They farmed the land, but I never took to it. Preferred riding a horse to driving a tractor. I run a few cattle on the place now to keep the grass down. Probably will increase my herd when I quit rodeoing."

"Are you planning on retiring soon?"

His shoulder brushed hers in a shrug. "Someday. Haven't really given much thought as to when."

With the sound of his husky voice beginning to relax

her, Shelby murmured, "Who takes care of your cattle while you're gone?"

"I stop in pretty regular, but I have a neighbor I pay to keep an eye on the place when I'm on the road."

"What's it like, traveling the—rodeo circuit? Isn't that what it's called?"

"Close enough." He shifted his shoulders more comfortably on the bed. "It's a lot of driving or flying when the schedule's tight and the rodeos are on opposite sides of the country. Being wound up tighter than a new spring when it's your turn to compete, and drained dry and limp as a wet rag once you're done. Eating breakfast in one state, dinner in another, trying, best we can, to hit as many rodeos as possible. Me, Pete and Clayton have been rodeoing together for about three years now. We take turns with the driving, spelling each other so we all have a chance to catch some sleep." He lifted a shoulder again. "That's about the size of it."

"Do you have family?" she asked, stifling a yawn.

He seemed to hesitate a moment, then replied, "A grandmother. But she's in a nursing home now."

"Is she ill?"

"Alzheimer's."

"How sad," Shelby said sympathetically, somewhat familiar with the disease. She stared at his profile a moment, her eyelids growing heavier and heavier. "Will you tell her about our marriage?"

"No. Probably not. Half the time she doesn't even recognize me. No need to confuse her more. Doubt she'd understand, anyway."

Though she couldn't see his expression, Shelby heard the regret in his voice, the sadness. Without thinking about the action, she reached over and placed her hand over his folded ones on his chest, giving them a squeeze. "I'm sorry, Troy," she murmured. "That must be hard on you."

Troy didn't say anything in response, couldn't. Just stared at the ceiling, trying his best to swallow the baseball-size wad of emotion that had risen to his throat. The comfort of her hand on his, the softness, the warmth as her body heat seeped slowly into his skin. He lay still as death, fearing if he moved she would, and not wanting to lose that contact. Finally he worked up the nerve to look at her. Her eyes were closed, her lips slightly parted and relaxed in sleep. Careful not to disturb her, he turned his hand over, opened it beneath hers and wove their fingers together.

An angel, he thought wistfully, giving her hand a gentle squeeze. Too bad he'd been handed a pitchfork at birth instead of a set of wings like hers. If he'd had the wings, maybe he could've flown with her, offered her more than just his name. Maybe he could have offered himself as a real husband to her and as a father to the child she carried.

As it was, the name he'd given her was sullied enough. No sense trying to tie her to the man folks claimed was responsible for dirtying the Jacobs name.

Sighing, he turned his face to the ceiling and closed his eyes.

He fell asleep with his fingers still woven through hers, steeped in her warmth and comforted by her touch.

Three

——

Troy was dreaming. He was sure he was, though there were no color or images in the dream. Just sound. An irritating scrape and clatter that began to work on his nerves. A metallic jiggling sound, as if someone was testing a lock. A squeak of hinges badly in need of oil. Then a loud, indignant inhalation of breath.

It was at that moment that Troy realized this was no dream.

But the realization came too late for him to react. A hand closed over his bare shoulder, blunt nails biting deep.

"What do you think you're doing in my daughter's bed? Get out! Out! Do you hear me? Out!"

There was a yank on his shoulder—a yank that lacked the strength required to budge a man of Troy's size—and Troy blinked open his eyes and met those of Shelby's father. He knew the man had to be her father. There was enough righteous indignation in his dark eyes to condemn a hundred men to hell for their sins.

Troy heard a soft moan beside him, then the fullness and curve of a hip bump up against his. Nervously he released the hand he still held and cleared his throat. "Shelby?" he said quietly, hauling himself to a sitting position. "Sweetheart, I think you better wake up."

The man staggered back as if Troy had punched him. His chest swelled, his nostrils flared and his neck turned a mottled red against the white collar that bound it. "Shelby Ruth Cannon," he ground out through clenched teeth. "You'd better have an explanation for this abomination. A very good one," he warned and spun to drop down onto one of the wicker chairs. He sat, his spine rigid, his hands splayed along thighs covered by unrelieved black gabardine, and drummed his fingers, waiting, his eyes narrowed on the window in front of him.

Shelby slowly pushed herself up on one elbow, swallowing hard as she stared at her father's profile. "Good morning, Daddy."

"Good morning?" he raged, snapping his head around to glare at her, his eyes shooting fire. "And what is good about a morning in which a father finds a strange man in his maiden daughter's bed?"

"He's not a stranger, Daddy," she said quietly. "He's my husband."

The man was on his feet so fast it made Troy's head swim.

"Husband!" he roared.

Though Troy felt inclined to offer an explanation of some kind, he thought it best to remain silent and let Shelby do the talking. After all, she was the one with all the answers, not him.

He felt the mattress shift slightly as she slipped from beneath the covers to stand beside it. "Yes, Daddy," she said as she pulled on her robe. "My husband. Troy and I were married yesterday."

"Married! Where?"

"Las Vegas."

The preacher sent Troy to hell with one damning look. "You took my daughter, my *innocent* daughter, to Las Vegas? What kind of man are you!"

"Daddy, please—" Shelby began.

He waved away her plea with an angry swipe of his hand. "You told your mother and I that you were going to Denver to spend Labor Day weekend with your cousin. I suppose that was a lie, as were the buying trips you've been taking for the past several months."

When Shelby guiltily dropped her gaze, he swelled his chest, his face a furious red as he turned his glare on Troy. Obviously he didn't like what he saw. "Is that your truck and trailer parked in the alley, and your horse tied to it?"

Troy refused to be cowed and met the man's eyes squarely. "Yes sir, it is."

"Am I to assume, then, that you are a cowboy?"

"I like to think so."

Troy's flippant response seemed to anger the man even more. He whirled to face his daughter. "I'll have the marriage annulled."

"Daddy!" Shelby cried in horror. "You can't!"

The preacher stared at her a long, gut-clenching moment, his eyes narrowing to suspicious slits. "And may I ask why not?"

Troy glanced at Shelby and watched the blood drain from her face.

"B-because—" She faltered for a moment, then gave her chin a stubborn lift. "Because I'm an adult and responsible for my own actions."

"Responsible?" her father said contemptuously. "And eloping with this—this *cowboy* is what you consider acting responsibly?"

Though the slight was directed at him, Troy ignored it,

more concerned with the effect the man's words were having on Shelby. Her face had gone from ghostly pale to beet-red in a matter of seconds, and she was trembling like a leaf. Though he'd had very little experience with pregnant women, he suspected emotional scenes like the current one being played out couldn't be good for her or her baby.

Hoping to intercede before any damage was done, he swung his legs across the bed and rose to his feet to stand beside her. Though the Reverend Daniel Cannon was tall, Troy was taller, and broader as well, a fact that he thought, for some stupid reason, might count in his favor.

But he'd failed to remember that he'd grown uncomfortable in the night and unfastened the waist of his jeans.

"For God's sake, man," the preacher cried, whirling away from the sight and covering his eyes. "Have you no sense of decency?"

Troy turned and quickly snagged up his zipper, shooting an apologetic look Shelby's way before turning back around.

"Mr. Cannon—"

The preacher stiffened, but kept his back to the two. "*Reverend* Cannon," he clarified with an imperious lift of his chin.

Troy set his jaw. "*Reverend* Cannon," he amended, putting the same inflection on the title the preacher had. "I'd appreciate it if you would lower your voice. You're upsetting my wife."

The man turned then, and the look of contempt in his eye was so strong Troy felt it like acid against his skin.

"In God's eyes, and *my* eyes, she isn't your wife and won't be," he added, turning to glower at Shelby, "until you are properly married in a church."

"But, Daddy—" Shelby cried.

He held up a hand, cutting her off. "I don't have time to discuss this further. I have a men's Bible class to teach."

He gave his waistcoat a tug, then marched for the door. At the threshold he stopped and looked back, singeing them both with a last, contemptuous look. "We'll discuss this at dinner tonight. Seven sharp. Don't be late." Before either could form a response, he slammed the door behind him with enough force to rattle the windows and set the art on the wall askew.

With the slam of the door reverberating in the small room, Troy crossed to the window, braced a wide hand on its frame and looked down below. Shelby knew by his frown that he was monitoring her father's departure.

She wanted desperately to throw something, anything. Rant, scream, chase down the stairs after her father and rail at him until she'd freed herself of the anger that burned through her.

But she didn't.

Instead she did as she'd learned to do years before—she took a deep breath...another...then yet another...suppressing the anger, the frustration, until it was nothing but a knot of burning tension in her stomach.

"I'm sorry, Troy. You didn't deserve that."

He lifted a shoulder. "Doesn't matter."

But it did matter. More, she suspected, than he would ever admit. "Yes, it does," she insisted. "He had no right to speak to you in that way."

His scowl deepening, he closed his hand into a fist on the window frame, making the muscles cord across his bare back. "He was angry. I was the natural target."

She took a step toward him, wanting to reassure him, wanting to take the sting out of her father's words, but stopped, unsure how best to do that. Lacing her fingers together to keep from reaching out to him and smoothing the tension from his back as she yearned to do, she squeezed her fingers together at her waist. "In spite of the things my father said, I know that you're a good man."

He snorted a laugh. "You wouldn't say that if you knew what I was thinking right now."

"Oh? And what are you thinking?

"That your father is a—" He clamped his lips together and shook his head, refusing to voice his thoughts aloud. "Never mind."

"He is a—what?" she prodded, taking a step closer. "A sanctimonious bastard?"

He snapped his head around to look at her. Whether his surprise was spawned by her accuracy in reading his thoughts or by hearing her speak so profanely, she wasn't sure. But it didn't matter. What mattered was convincing him that he'd done nothing wrong. He was simply an innocent bystander caught in the cross fire of a battle begun long before he appeared on the scene. "That *is* what you were thinking, wasn't it?"

Frowning, he turned to face the window again. "Close enough."

"Knowing you harbor such thoughts about my father doesn't make me think any less of you. I've had similar ones over the years."

"How old are you?"

Startled by the unexpected question, Shelby frowned at his back. "Twenty-three. Why?"

He snapped his head around to peer at her. "Twenty-three?" he repeated in dismay. "And you let your old man get by with treating you like a two-year-old?" With a snort of disgust, he shook his head and turned back to the window.

She lifted her chin. "He's simply protective, a trait that I find suffocating at times but one that I understand. My sister put our family through hell with her transgressions, and I don't intend to cause my parents any more pain with mine."

"Your sister's transgressions?" he repeated, turning to

look at her. "And what did she do?" he asked sarcastically. "Steal a dollar from the collection plate?"

"More like $40,000."

Shocked that he'd unknowingly hit the nail on the head, Troy could only stare.

"Yes, $40,000," she replied, responding to his surprised look. "She served as the church secretary and embezzled the money from the church treasury. Her thievery wasn't discovered until after she had run away with—"

"A cowboy," he said for her with a weary sigh, remembering the disgust with which the preacher had spoken the word.

"Yes, a cowboy. She had dated Marshall for more than a year, and though my father didn't approve of the relationship, he didn't forbid her to see him, thinking she would, in time, outgrow the infatuation. Unfortunately, she didn't. Instead she stole money from the church and ran away with him." She caught her lower lip between her teeth, her eyes filling with tears. "You have no idea the pain, the humiliation, her actions caused my family, especially my father. I swore then that I'd never hurt him similarly."

Troy blew out a long breath, wondering if this nightmare could get any worse. "Why, when my profession must have been obvious to you, did you choose me, a cowboy, as a husband to bring home to your father? Surely you must have known how he would react?"

The question dried her tears and put a flush of anger in her cheeks. "I didn't choose you because you were a cowboy."

"Then why *did* you choose me?" he asked, his anger rising to meet hers.

"Because I was desperate!"

He tossed up a hand. "Well, thanks a whole hell of a lot," he muttered irritably.

Realizing too late that she had insulted him, Shelby covered her face with her hands. "I didn't mean that the way it sounded," she said wearily, then dropped her hands with a sigh to look at him again. "Yes, I was desperate. I had been sitting in that diner for hours, trying to think what I should do. Then you walked in."

"Surely there were other men before me? Hell," he said, remembering the night's events. "The Corley brothers were leaving as I walked in! Why didn't you ask one of them?"

"Because it didn't occur to me."

"Oh, so you were looking for a sucker, and I was the first man through the door who fit the bill?"

She curled her hands into fists at her sides. "That wasn't the case, at all. It hadn't occurred to me to ask anyone to marry me until I overheard you say you might have to sell your horse. Upon hearing that, I thought we might be able to help each other out of otherwise hopeless situations."

"My situation's not hopeless," he muttered defensively.

"Well, mine is!" she cried.

Troy had to agree. Especially after having met her father and hearing her reasons for needing a father for the child she carried. The reminder sent guilt stabbing through him for the thoughtless comments he'd made. "I'm sorry," he mumbled.

"You have nothing to be sorry for. You've done nothing but try to assist me in avoiding causing my father any further humiliation. For that alone I'm grateful.

"And I'm sorry that my father was rude to you," she added. "His anger is misguided and should be directed at me, not you. I certainly never meant for you to take the blame for my mistake."

He heaved a sigh and propped his chin on his braced arm. "I suppose he'll be dishing out more of the same tonight, huh?"

"Yes," she replied, and turned for the kitchen, her robe

whipping around her bare ankles. "But thankfully you won't be around to hear it."

Distracted a moment by the span of bare leg he'd glimpsed, he didn't immediately register her comment. When he did, he straightened and stared after her. *She didn't expect him to stay?* He gave his head a shake, sure that he had misunderstood her. There was no way in hell she was going to let him off the hook this easily. Not that he was anxious to go another round with her old man. He just couldn't believe she didn't expect him to stick around for round two.

Frowning, he headed for the kitchen. "But your father specifically said that we were *both* to be there for dinner tonight."

"Yes, he did," she agreed as she pulled a can of coffee grounds from the cupboard. "But you've already fulfilled your end of our agreement. I won't ask anything more of you. Would you like some coffee?" she asked, tipping the can toward him.

"Yeah," he said slowly, surprised that she could even think about putting something in her stomach. Personally, he felt as if he'd been fed through a meat grinder, taking the heat for another man's sins. Resenting that wrongful association more than a little, he turned and braced his back against the counter, folding his arms across his chest, scowling as she measured grounds into the coffeemaker's basket.

Her hands were those of a lady, he noted absently as he watched her fill the pot with water. Soft, smooth skin. Long, graceful fingers. Almond-shaped nails painted the same shell-pink he'd noticed on her toes during the drive to Las Vegas. He couldn't help wondering, as he watched her work, how such a fine lady had become involved with a man with the morals of an alley cat? A man who would leave her high and dry when he found out she was pregnant?

But was Troy any better than the man who had abandoned her? He was, after all, planning on leaving her, too, he reminded himself.

Feeling the guilt eat a little deeper, he shifted his gaze to stare at her profile. "I suppose my absence will create more problems for you."

"Probably." She switched on the coffeemaker, then shifted to open the refrigerator. "But don't worry about it. This isn't your problem." She pulled out a carton of eggs and held them up in invitation. "Scrambled or fried?"

"Scrambled." He watched silently as she set out five eggs, then pulled a bowl from the cupboard. Though she was putting on a hell of a performance, as he studied her more closely he could see the level of nerves she was hiding. The tiny worry lines on her forehead. The tension around her mouth. The slight trembling in her hands. Obviously, the prospect of facing her father again terrified her. Hell, it would him, and he was bigger, meaner, and had a lot tougher hide than Shelby.

Frowning, he plucked a mug from the row of brass hooks beneath the cupboard. "What will you tell him?"

She glanced his way, her forehead knit in puzzlement. "About what?"

"About me." He poured coffee into the mug, then turned, leaning back against the counter again. "How will you explain my absence?"

She hesitated a moment, then lifted a shoulder and turned away, cracking an egg on the edge of the bowl. "I'll just tell him the truth."

"And what would that be?" he asked, certain that the "truth" was that her new husband was a loser, just as her father had assumed, and had skipped out on her at the first sign of trouble.

"That you had a rodeo to compete in," she said as if stating the obvious.

It *was* the truth, he reminded himself as he blew on the steaming coffee. He did have a rodeo to compete in. But if that was the case, then why the hell did he feel so guilty for ducking out on her?

You did your part, he reminded himself firmly. You married her and came home with her to meet her father as agreed. End of bargain.

He took a sip of coffee and attempted to swallow the guilt he couldn't seem to shake. But it remained, giving the coffee a bitter taste. He was tired, he told himself. If he wasn't, there was no way in hell he would ever feel guilty for a situation not of his doing.

Frowning, he glanced her way. "Would you mind if I stayed for a couple of hours and tried to get some more sleep before I head out?"

"Not at all," she replied as she whisked the eggs to a froth. "I have to open the shop in a little while, so you'll have the apartment to yourself. Sleep as long as you want."

Shelby heard the soft thump on the floor overhead and knew the sound was Troy's feet hitting the floor as he climbed from her bed. Though she'd been listening for the sound all morning, she tensed upon hearing it, knowing it signified that he would be coming down soon. That he would be leaving.

And, God help her, she thought, feeling the panic rising, she didn't want him to leave. The very thought of him doing so made her want to run upstairs and throw herself against that broad chest of his and beg him to stay.

She supposed it was because of the comfort, the added strength, she'd experienced with him at her side that morning, when she'd confronted her father. A comfort and strength she would all but kill for at dinner that night when she had to face her father again.

You're just being selfish, she scolded silently. Troy had been more than generous in allowing her to use his name and coming home with her to meet her father. She shouldn't expect any more from him. The rest she would have to deal with alone.

She picked up a feather duster and moved around her shop, dusting knickknacks that didn't need dusting and fluffing pillows that didn't need fluffing, trying her best not to listen to the sounds overhead, trying not to think about the fact that he would be leaving soon.

But when the water pipes groaned, she froze, aware that the sound was coming from the bathroom in her apartment. She glanced up at the ceiling, gulping as she listened to the muffled sounds of Troy's movements, knowing that he was preparing to take a shower. Squeezing her eyes shut, she tried not to envision him there, in her bathroom, stripping off his jeans and stepping naked beneath the shower's spray.

But the image was there behind her closed lids, a shadowed impression first drawn when she'd stolen a peek at him the night before, watching as he'd stripped off his shirt and boots before crawling into bed beside her. An image enhanced by morning's light and turning to vivid Technicolor when, bare chested and wearing nothing but his unbuttoned jeans, he'd risen from her bed to stand beside her to face her father. Those broad shoulders, that muscled chest, those corded arms. The dark smattering of hair that swirled around his navel before disappearing beneath the waist of his jeans. Though she didn't know what lay beneath the faded jeans, she could well imagine how he'd look completely naked. Narrow hips, rounded buttocks, muscled thighs and calves...

Groaning, she dropped her chin, pressing the flat of her

hand against her forehead. This is sick, she told herself miserably. She shouldn't be harboring lustful thoughts about Troy. Heavens! He was all but a stranger!

Yet, he was her husband.

She firmed her lips and forced her hand into motion again, sweeping the feather duster along the colorful glass shade of a Tiffany lamp. He wasn't her *real* husband, she reminded herself. Theirs was a business agreement. Five thousand dollars in exchange for his name. A mutually beneficial arrangement for both parties.

Then why did the thought of him leaving make her feel like crying? Like throwing herself at his mercy and begging him to stay?

"Good mornin'."

At the sound of his sleep-roughened voice, she whirled, clutching the feather duster to her breasts. The sight of him standing there at the foot of the rear staircase, his wide shoulders filling the narrow space, stole what was left of her breath. He looked so much taller than she remembered, and bigger, too. Much bigger. And his hair seemed darker than it had earlier that morning, but that was probably because it was still damp from the shower.

But it was his eyes that held her in place and seemed to tie her tongue in knots. A soft blue-gray, they were filled with such an endearing blend of shyness and compassion that she felt tears clog her throat. Oh, why couldn't she have chosen a man like Troy to fall in love with? she cried silently. Why had she fallen for a man like Derrick? A man who was all polish and no substance?

He cleared his throat and shuffled his feet uneasily, making her aware that she was staring and had yet to return his greeting. Her cheeks flaming, she darted behind the counter. "Did you sleep well?" she asked, snatching up a stack of invoices to hide the fact that her hands were shaking.

"I can sleep most anywhere."

Remembering how his feet had hung off the end of her bed, she murmured an apology. "I'm sorry. My bed is rather small for a man of your size."

He chuckled, the sound coming from deep in his chest and sending a shiver dancing down her spine.

"Beats the hell out of the second seat in Pete's dually."

"Dually?" she repeated, turning to look at him in confusion.

"An extended cab truck with dual rear wheels. Like the one I drive."

"Oh."

He started across the room and she quickly turned back around, setting aside the invoices and pulling her checkbook from beneath the counter. Drawing in a fortifying breath, she flipped the book open, knowing she had to get this over with quickly, before she was on her knees begging him to stay.

"I know you're probably anxious to be on your way," she began as she reached for a pen. But before she could touch pen to paper, he stopped beside her, bringing with him the scent of roses.

Roses?

She faltered, the pen slipping from suddenly weak fingers as she recognized the fragrance as that of the scented bar of soap she kept in her shower. The realization that he had used the same soap to shower with as she had used only hours before spoke of an intimacy that sent her pulse racing.

Shifting away from him, she picked up the pen again, leaned over and began to fill in the blanks. "My bank is just down the street," she told him, hoping he didn't notice the quaver in her voice. "You can cash this there as you're leaving town." She signed her name with a flourish and tore the check from the book, then turned. Forcing a grateful smile, she held the check out to him. "I really appreciate what you've done for me, Troy. For my baby."

Frowning, he dropped his gaze to the check and took a step back, rubbing his hand down his thigh. "I can't take your money, Shelby."

Pursing her lips, she caught his hand and flipped it over, pressing the check across his palm. "We made a deal," she reminded him sternly, forcing his fingers to close around the document. "Your name for five thousand dollars. You upheld your end of the bargain. Now I'm upholding mine."

Troy glanced up, meeting her gaze, seeing the stubbornness in her blue eyes. But beneath it he saw the worry, the fear. It was at that moment he knew he wasn't going anywhere, at least not until the appointed dinner with her parents was over. "But that's just it," he said. "I haven't upheld my end of the bargain. At least, not in your daddy's eyes."

With a huff of breath, she dropped her hand from his and turned back to the counter. "Don't worry about my father," she said tersely as she picked up the stack of receipts again. She tamped them firmly against the countertop, straightening them. "I can handle things from here."

He stared at her profile, wondering how someone who looked as if a strong wind might blow her over, who quaked when confronted with her father's anger, could sound so tough, so sure of herself. "Really? And how do you plan to do that?"

Her shoulders drooped slightly, but she quickly caught herself and squared them again. Slipping the receipts into the checkbook, she closed the cover. "I don't know just yet. But that's my problem, not yours."

Troy glanced at the check she'd given him, suspecting the amount represented her life savings, money that she could use for herself and the baby. Money he didn't need—

a part of their bargain that he'd hidden behind to keep secret his own reasons for agreeing to marry her. "You
know," he said slowly, "five thousand dollars is a lot of
money to pay for just a man's name."

"It was the arrangement we made. I'm satisfied with it."

He shook his head, then angled it to look at her. "I don't
know that I am. I doubt I'll be able to sleep at night, knowing that I've taken advantage of a woman."

She huffed another breath and turned, brushing past him.
"You aren't taking advantage of me. I have your name,
and that's what I wanted, what we agreed to."

He trailed her, weaving his way down the aisles shaped
by carefully arranged antiques. "But I thought the idea was
to convince your father that you're really married?"

"Well, it is," she said, spinning to face him, her frustration obvious.

Frowning, he lifted a hand to scratch his head. "Then
why are you packing me off so fast? Wouldn't it make
better sense for me to hang around long enough to go to
this dinner tonight?"

Before Shelby could respond, the bell on the shop's door
chimed, and they both turned to look in that direction. An
old woman hobbled in, using her cane to close the door
behind her.

"Oh, no," Shelby moaned under her breath.

"What's wrong?"

"That's Maybelle Porter," she said miserably, keeping
her voice low. "The biggest gossip in town." She forced
a smile and lifted a hand in greeting. "Good afternoon,
Mrs. Porter," she called out. "I'll be right with you."
Turning back to Troy, she whispered urgently, "Please.
Just go. I don't need your assistance any longer."

But Troy wasn't so sure that she didn't. He'd seen the
way her father had treated her, had felt the razor-sharp cut
of the man's tongue himself, and knew that Shelby was a

long way from accomplishing what she'd hoped to accomplish by marrying him. But how could he stay when she seemed hellbent on his leaving?

Hearing the tap of the old woman's cane drawing nearer, he glanced in her direction…and saw the opportunity he needed. He ducked around Shelby and headed straight for Maybelle Porter. "I don't believe we've met," he said and grabbed her hand. "I'm Troy Jacobs. Shelby's husband."

The woman stared up at him in bewilderment, as he pumped her hand up and down. "Husband?" she repeated, then peered around him to frown at Shelby. "I don't remember reading about an engagement in the paper."

Troy released the woman's hand to draw Shelby to his side, wrapping an arm at her waist. "Everything happened so fast we haven't had a chance to make a proper announcement yet. Have we, sweetheart?" he asked, smiling down at her.

Stunned, Shelby could only stare at him, her heart and mind frozen on the fact that Troy had introduced himself as her husband. And to the town gossip, no less.

He gave her waist a squeeze. "Have we, sweetheart?" he prodded.

"N-no," she stammered, pulling herself from her daze. "No, we haven't."

The woman eyed the two suspiciously. "Seems kind of sudden, if you ask me."

"Oh, it was fast all right," Troy agreed. He hugged Shelby against his side, smiling down at her again. "First time I laid eyes on this little filly, I knew she was the woman for me. Now, if you ladies will excuse me," he said politely, taking his leave, "I need to find a place to exercise my horse. It was nice meeting you, Mrs. Porter." When he reached the rear of the shop, he stopped and turned. "Oh, and, sweetheart," he called to Shelby. "Don't worry. I'll be back in plenty of time to make it to your parents' for dinner tonight."

Four

"Are you pregnant?"

Shelby choked on her iced tea. Though she'd been waiting all evening for her father to broach the subject of her marriage to Troy, she'd hoped to avoid *that* particular question.

Troy glanced at Shelby in concern as she coughed, her face a brilliant red, then leaned to pat her on the back. "I certainly hope so," he said, answering for her. "We're anxious to get our family started, aren't we, sweetheart?"

With her napkin pressed against her mouth, Shelby stared at Troy, her eyes wide in disbelief. Feeling the urgent prod of his finger against her spine, she quickly nodded her agreement. "Y-yes," she stammered hoarsely, then cleared her throat. "Yes, we are."

"Children are such a blessing," her mother said, smiling her approval. "Shelby has certainly been the light of our lives."

"More like a floodlight, at the moment," her father groused, tossing his napkin onto his plate in disgust.

"Daniel, please..." Marian Cannon began.

The preacher brought his fist down on the table, making the silverware rattle. "Don't, 'Daniel' me," he raged, his temper rising out of nowhere. "News of her marriage is already all over town. Wasn't the shame your sister brought on this family enough?" he demanded of Shelby. "Didn't you learn anything from the hell she put this family through? Weren't you forced to sacrifice your own college education so that her debts could be repaid?"

Troy could almost feel Shelby's slim shoulders bending beneath the guilt being heaped upon them.

"I'm sorry, Daddy, but—"

"But, nothing!" he roared. "As a spiritual leader in this community, I'm expected to set an example, as is my family. And what kind of example am I setting when my own daughters' behavior is that of thieves and harlots? It was bad enough that your sister stole from the church, then ran off, leaving us to deal with her sins, but then you had to run off to Las Vegas, of all places, and marry some—" he churned a hand in the air as if searching for a word vile enough to describe Troy "—cowboy!" he finished furiously. "How could you!"

"Do you have something against cowboys?" Troy asked pointedly, hoping to shift the man's anger away from Shelby and onto himself. "Or is it just me?"

"Nothing other than that you are all a tobacco-spitting, woman-chasing, shiftless breed of men who foolishly risk your lives trying to prove your manhood by pitting your strength and what little wits you have against some wild animal."

Shelby flattened her hands on the table, her face flushed with fury as she pushed herself on her feet. "You may feel you have the right to speak to me in such a manner, but you have no right to insult my husband in such a way. Let's go, Troy.''

Though relieved to see Shelby finally stand up to her father, Troy caught her hand and pulled her back down to her chair. ''He has a right to state his opinion,'' he said, then shifted his gaze to her father's, ''as I do to state mine.''

''But, Troy—''

He squeezed her hand, silencing her. ''Reverend Cannon,'' he said, never once breaking eye contact with the preacher, ''you said this morning that in God's eyes, and your eyes, Shelby isn't my wife and won't be until we are properly married in a church.''

The preacher reared back in his chair, sticking his thumbs in the armholes of his waistcoat and swelling his chest. ''That's exactly what I said, and I meant every word. Without the blessings of the church, your relationship with my daughter, in my eyes, is adulterous.''

''Is that so?''

''Yes, that's so.''

''Then I'd like to rectify that situation,'' Troy said, his voice a deathly calm. ''And I'd like *you* to perform the ceremony.''

The minister jerked upright. ''Wh-what?'' he sputtered.

''You name the date and the time, and Shelby and I will repeat our vows again for you and whoever else you think needs to hear them.'' He rose then, drawing Shelby to her feet, as well. He turned to her mother and extended his hand. ''Thank you for the dinner, Mrs. Cannon. It's been a while since I've enjoyed a home-cooked meal.''

Her expression incredulous, Marion Cannon took his hand and shook it slowly. ''Th-thank you, Troy.''

He turned and, with a nod to Shelby's father, led a speechless Shelby to the door.

* * *

"Why did you offer to do such a thing?" Shelby whispered furiously as she stormed down the sidewalk a step ahead of Troy.

"What thing?" he asked innocently.

"Why did you offer to marry me again? We *are* married. Remember?"

"Yeah, I remember. But the whole point of my being here is to convince your father that we are man and wife." He shrugged a shoulder, though Shelby didn't see the gesture. "Seemed as if the surest and fastest way to convince the man was to agree to repeat our vows for him."

"Ughh," Shelby groaned furiously, whirling to face him. "But it isn't fair!"

Troy wrinkled his nose in confusion. "What isn't fair?"

"Our agreement was that you would marry me, and you've already done that. And now you have to marry me again!"

"I don't remember us spelling out any particulars."

She spun away, folding her arms across her chest, to glare at the dark street. Behind her, Troy began to chuckle.

"What is so funny?" she snapped peevishly.

"Did you see his face when I offered to let him do the honors?"

In spite of her anger, Shelby felt a bubble of laughter swell inside her as she remembered the shocked look on her father's face. "Beat him to the button, didn't you?" she said, laughing softly, pleased that someone had at last managed to render her father speechless.

"Sure did," he agreed, and draped an arm around her shoulders, heading her back toward her shop.

As they walked down the moonlit sidewalk in companionable silence, increasing the distance from her father's house and decreasing the distance to her own, Shelby's pleasure slowly melted away as she realized what Troy had set himself up for. "I appreciate what you're trying to do,

Troy, but you don't have to go through with this. This is my problem, not yours."

Troy shook his head. Twelve hours ago he might have taken the out she offered, but the situation had become a personal one for him, made so by her father. And Troy Jacobs never walked away from a fight, not his own, nor anyone else's when he felt they were the underdog. "Nope," he said firmly. "I'm in for the long haul."

Shelby stopped, catching him by the elbow and stopping him, too, her eyes gleaming with tears. "But this isn't what you agreed to, at all."

He shrugged a shoulder. "No, but then, as I said, we never spelled out the particulars, did we?"

She tightened her fingers on his arm, her nails digging deep. "I won't hold you to our agreement, and I won't think less of you if you choose to drive away right now. I swear, I won't."

Troy could see that she meant every word, but then how could she possibly think less of him when she knew nothing about him in the first place. "Less of nothing isn't much," he replied dryly.

Pursing her lips, she dropped her hand from his arm and tucked it beneath her breasts again. The action thrust her breasts up and afforded him a small peek at the dark valley that lay between and the twin swells of flesh that shadowed it. Some women might have used the action on purpose, as a ploy of sorts. But Shelby didn't strike him as the type to flaunt.

"I know enough," she stated emphatically. "I know that you're kind and thoughtful and honorable. And I know that—"

Troy held up his hands. "Whoa. Wait a minute. You know no such thing."

"I most certainly do," she argued furiously. "If you weren't kind, you wouldn't have agreed to marry me in the first place. And if you weren't thoughtful, you wouldn't have ordered that bridal bouquet for me in Las Vegas. And if you weren't honorable, you wouldn't be standing here, right now, arguing with me! So there!'' She spun and marched down the sidewalk, her arms pumping at her sides, the hem of her calf-length skirt swishing around her legs.

Troy watched her, pleased that she was showing a little backbone, displaying some of that anger he suspected she kept all bottled up inside. And, Lord, but wasn't she beautiful when she let fly with a little of that temper? It turned her blue eyes to fire, making them snap and sparkle like summer lightning, stained her cheeks a healthy rose and swelled her chest, causing her breasts to rise and fall beneath her loose-fitting blouse, until it was all he could do to keep his hands in his pockets and himself from touching her.

But wasn't it a damned shame that she was stupid, too, he thought sadly. And blind. Troy Jacobs, honorable? Troy Jacobs, thoughtful? Troy Jacobs, kind? No way.

But Shelby was all those things, and because she was, he was determined to do whatever it took to help her convince her daddy and the town of Dunning that she was a married woman and he was the father of the baby she carried.

He watched her march down nearly half a block before she realized that he wasn't following her. She stopped and turned, frowning at him. ''Well? Are you coming, or not?'' she whispered impatiently, in deference to the houses that lined the sidewalk and any ears that might be listening.

That she would worry what the neighbors thought spoke volumes about her sense of propriety and made Troy want to take a little of that starch out of her drawers. ''Coming where?'' he called out to her.

''Well, home, of course.''

''Only if I can be underneath this time,'' he replied, raising his voice a notch for the neighbors' benefit. "I was on top last night, remember?"

Her mouth fell open, then snapped shut with a click as she looked quickly around to make sure no one had overheard his lewd comment. Firming her lips she marched back down the sidewalk. "Would you please keep your voice down?" she whispered furiously. "Someone might get the wrong idea."

"Hell," he said rakishly, and slung an arm around her shoulders and turned her for home. "We're married, aren't we? How could anyone find something wrong with a man sharing a bed with his wife?"

But they didn't share a bed that night. As soon as they'd arrived back at Shelby's apartment, Troy told her he had to leave in order to make it to the rodeo in Pecos on time.

Shelby had watched him pack his gear and load his horse, blaming the tears that burned her throat on the emotional swings she'd discovered went along with her pregnancy.

And when he'd stood beside his truck and scribbled his cell phone number on the back of a fuel receipt before giving it to her, and instructed her to call him when her father had set the date and time for their wedding, she was grateful for the darkness that hid the tears brimming in her eyes.

But as she watched his taillights disappear when he made the turn from the alley behind her shop and onto the main street of Dunning, she didn't even try to stop the tears that streaked down her face.

She cried because she knew he was all the things she'd claimed him to be. Kind. Thoughtful, Honorable.

But most of all, she cried because she already missed him.

* * *

Troy lay in the loft bed in his trailer, thrumming his fingers against his chest, listening to the rain pinging on the roof overhead, sleep the furthest thing from his mind. He glanced at the cell phone lying on the mattress beside him, reached for it, then snatched his hand back, frowning.

He wouldn't call her, he told himself. He had no reason to call her. Doing so would suggest a relationship that didn't exist. Couldn't exist.

Afraid that if he didn't call someone, though, he'd weaken and call Shelby, he snatched up the phone and punched in a number. He listened through three rings, his frown turning to a scowl.

"Hello?"

The fact that Pete sounded a little out of breath took Troy by surprise. "Pete? What the hell are you doing? Running laps?"

"No. Doing push-ups," his friend replied, laughing, then yelped. "Hey! What did you hit me for? It's only Troy."

"What?" Troy asked in confusion.

"I wasn't talking to you," Pete snapped impatiently. "I was talking to Carol. Come on, baby. Don't be mad."

Rolling his eyes, Troy dropped his head to his pillow, cradling the phone to his ear. "I take it I interrupted something."

"Definitely something," Pete agreed suggestively, then yelped again. "Dammit, Carol, would you stop hitting me!"

"Listen," Troy said, wishing he'd never made the call. "I'll catch you later."

"Don't hang up now!" Pete cried. "Hell. The damage is done. Carol's already locked herself in the bathroom. It'll take a good hour for her to cool off enough for me to even think about approaching her again. Women," he muttered disagreeably.

"You can't live with 'em, and you can't live without 'em," the two men said in unison, then shared a laugh.

"Well, now that you've put a hitch in my sex life," Pete said with a sigh, "why'd you call?"

"Just checkin' in. Heard from Clayton?"

"Nope. But he can stay gone as long as needed. I've got everything under control here."

"Except Carol," Troy reminded him.

"She's just a little sensitive, is all," Pete explained. "Doesn't want anybody to know we're living in sin over here at Clayton's. Because of her students, and all. 'Course I told her that I'd marry her and make an honest woman of her, but—"

Troy sat straight up in the bed, swearing when he bumped his head sharply on the trailer's low ceiling. "Did you say *marry* her?" he asked, rubbing the sore spot on his head.

"Shor' 'nuf did," Pete replied proudly. "Just waitin' on her to set a date. But you know how women are. Gotta plan out every detail, right down to the number of flower petals in her bouquet."

Troy frowned, thinking of Shelby standing at the reception desk at the chapel in Las Vegas, her chin quivering, her voice breaking, shaking her head each time the receptionist suggested a different frill for their trumped-up wedding. "A woman deserves for her wedding day to be special," Troy said in Carol's defense...or was it in Shelby's?

A sharp tapping sound crossed the airwaves, making Troy pull the phone away from his ear in annoyance.

"Hello?" Pete said, tapping a finger again against the phone's mouthpiece. "Hello? Is this Troy Jacobs I'm a talkin' to?"

Troy scowled, putting the phone back to his ear. "You know damn good and well it is," he grumbled.

"Well, when did you become an authority on a woman's needs?"

"Yesterday, when I got married."

"What! Married? You? To who?"

Troy groaned at the shotgun questions Pete fired at him, wishing he'd kept his mouth shut. "It's not a real marriage," he said uneasily. "I'm just sort of lending this lady my name for a while."

"Well, hell, Troy, are you married or not?"

Troy puffed his cheeks and slowly released a breath. "Married."

"To who?"

"You don't know her. She's just a woman I met in a diner."

"You married a woman you met in a diner. Where are you, Troy? I'm coming to get you."

If he didn't feel so miserable, Troy would have laughed at the panic he heard in Pete's voice. "You don't need to come and get me. I'm okay."

"You're okay? You tell me that you've just married a complete stranger, a woman that you picked up in some diner, and I'm supposed to believe that you're all right? Not in this lifetime, buddy."

"I didn't pick her up. She picked me up. See, she's pregnant and—"

"Pregnant! Geez, Troy, have you lost your mind?"

Frustrated, Troy raked his fingers through his hair. "It's not what you think. She just needed a name for her baby. Her father's the preacher in town and she—"

"Preacher! You married a pregnant preacher's daughter and you aren't even the father of the baby? Where are you, Troy? I swear I'm coming to get you."

Fighting for patience, Troy dragged a hand down his face. "If you'd just listen—"

"Listen, hell! I'm having a heart attack and you're telling me to listen? Carol! Get in here! You're not going to believe this!''

"Don't tell Carol," Troy begged, then groaned as he heard Pete repeating the story to Carol.

"Troy?"

He sighed wearily as the sound of Carol's voice. "Yeah," he said miserably, "it's me."

"Did you really marry a pregnant preacher's daughter?"

"Yes," he said, and fell back on the bed, thumping a frustrated fist against his forehead. "But it's not at all like Pete says. I'm not crazy."

"Well, I don't care what Pete says. *I* think you are the most wonderful, generous person in the whole, wide world."

"Now don't go making me into something I'm not," he warned, uncomfortable with the admiration he heard in her voice. "I'm just doing the lady a favor."

"Favor or not, I think you are really something special, Troy Jacobs."

Embarrassed, Troy changed the subject. "I gotta go, but tell Pete something for me, will you?"

"What?"

"Tell him I took second place tonight. I think my luck's beginning to change."

Before Carol could reply, Troy broke the connection and dropped the phone on the mattress by his side.

He wasn't anybody's hero, he told himself sourly. And he wasn't crazy, either, as Pete had suggested. He was just doing Shelby a favor. Period.

Afraid he'd miss Shelby's call to tell him the date and time for their proposed wedding, Troy nearly wore a hole in his back pocket over the next several days carrying his cell phone around. He did manage to wear the letters clean off the on button, though, testing to make sure the battery was still charged. He was that worried he'd miss her call.

He'd even paid a cowboy ten bucks to hold his phone for him while he made his run at the rodeo in Mesquite on Saturday night, repeating the instructions twice to make sure the cowboy knew how to operate the device before he reluctantly entrusted it to his care.

The phone didn't ring while he was making his run, but in spite of his lack of concentration, Troy did manage to pick up the money in his go-around, throwing his steer in 5.3 seconds. And he had more than a fair shot at the rodeo's fastest time, if no one beat his record at Sunday's performance.

Restless, he decided not to wait around for the final results, but headed his truck and trailer down I-20 and home. He arrived just before midnight, unloaded Danny Boy and let him out in the pasture near the barn. With a full moon lighting his way to the house, he hopped up the porch steps, unlocked the door and pushed it open...then took a quick step back, curling his nose when the musty smell of a house closed up too long rushed out to greet him.

Firming his lips, he braced his hands on his hips and stared into the dark interior. Not so long ago, the house wouldn't have been dark upon his return, and the smells that greeted him would have been pleasant ones. Mouth-watering scents of pies baking in the oven. Apricot, more often than not, because his grandmother knew it was his favorite. Granny would have been in the kitchen watching for his arrival and would have swung the screen door wide in welcome. Laughing and crying at the same time, she would have caught his cheeks between her gnarled, arthritic hands and given him a big smack on the lips, then hustled him to the table and plied him with sweets, smiling and patting his hand while he ate his pie and caught her up with his news.

Dragging an arm across his damp eyes, Troy turned away from the dark house and shoved his hands deep into his pockets as he shuffled his way back across the drive and to the pasture where he'd unloaded Danny Boy when he'd first arrived. With a full moon illuminating the pasture, he hitched a boot on the gate's lowest rung, his arms along the highest and dropped his chin on his crossed wrists.

Feeling more lonesome than he had in a long, long time, he watched Danny Boy trot across the pasture to join the other horses. The horse nickered as he neared the small herd, then stopped in front of the mare and butted her nose with his. A kiss of sorts, Troy supposed and felt a stab of envy.

He'd never kissed Shelby. Not after the wedding ceremony in Las Vegas and not when he'd left for Pecos, though the desire to do so had been there both times. A sense of longing welled up inside him as he remembered her standing beside his truck as he'd prepared to leave. She'd looked so lost, so abandoned, looking up at him, her eyes swimming with tears. He'd been tempted to kiss her right then and there, to take her in his arms and just hold her.

But he hadn't.

And now he was left with a huge knot of need and feeling restless and irritable, wishing he was back in that poor excuse of a bed of hers with her curled against his side. He inhaled deeply and closed his eyes, drawing the memory of her body snugged up against his, the comfort, the heat. Roses. Her scent. Permeating every inch of the tiny apartment. The pillow he slept on. The soap he'd used in her shower. Even now he could smell the roses. Her. And wished with all his heart he had it all to do over again, because this time he *would* kiss her. He would stroke a hand along the creamy smooth flesh of her shoulder and slip a hand over one of those sumptuous breasts and close his fingers around her softness. He would bury himself deep inside her and relieve this ache she'd left him with.

Realizing the direction his thoughts were taking him, he spun away from the fence, swearing. For God's sake! What was wrong with him? He had no right to harbor such thoughts about Shelby. She was a nice woman. A lady. Despite her current circumstances, he knew that to be true. She wasn't interested in pursuing a relationship with him, any more than he was interested in pursuing one with her. She'd needed a name, and he'd agreed to provide one for her. End of story.

But if that was so, then why was his cell phone burning a hole in his back pocket as it had been for the past two days, just begging for him to pick it up and give her a call, just so he could hear the sound of her voice again?

He groaned, raking his hands through his hair as he lifted his face to stare at the moon. More than his next meal, he wished he had his grandmother to talk to, so he could discuss with her the tangled feelings he had for Shelby. Wiser than an owl and not a bit shy about offering her opinion, his granny would have put a hot iron on his problems and straightened them out for him in nothing flat.

But he didn't have his granny to talk to anymore. He didn't have anyone. Not even his traveling buddies.

He just had a wife.

A wife in name only, and one who needed him, he reminded himself, if only for a few short months.

Hoping he wasn't making a mistake, he eased the cell phone from his back pocket and stared at it for a full minute before working up the nerve to punch in her number.

She answered on the third ring with a muffled, "Hello."

"Shelby? Did I wake you?"

"Troy?" she said sleepily. "Is that you?"

"Yeah," he said, and inhaled deeply, bracing a hand low

on his hip as he tipped his face up to stare at the moon. "It's me. How are you?"

"F-fine," she stammered, then asked uncertainly, "Are you okay?"

"Yeah." Digging for an excuse for calling, he said, "I won my go-round tonight. I think my run of bad luck has just about played out."

"That's wonderful, Troy," she said, and he thought that was real enthusiasm he heard in her voice, not forced.

"Might even have a chance for more," he added, "if nobody beats my time tomorrow."

"Are you still in Pecos?"

"No. I finished up there last night. Took second place and the purse that went along with it. I rode in Mesquite tonight." He glanced at the illuminated face of his watch and bit back a groan. "Or rather last night. I'm sorry, Shelby," he said in apology. "I shouldn't have called so late."

"No," she said, sounding more alert now. "I'm glad you called."

"You are?"

"Yes. And I'm thrilled that you and Danny Boy are doing so well."

Troy decided right then and there that the money he had won meant nothing to him when compared to the pride he heard in Shelby's voice.

"Are you in bed?" he asked, trying not to think how she'd look there, wearing her prim little nightgown, her hair all mussed from sleep.

"W-well, yes," she said in surprise. "Aren't you?"

"No."

"Where are you?"

"At home. Just got here. There's a full moon tonight, and I'm standing out here by the fence, watching Danny

Boy flirt with the mare. At the moment she's pretending to ignore him."

She laughed softly, and the sound sent a warmth rushing through him that settled in a knot in his groin.

"Oh, I'd like to see that," she said. "I imagine he's glad to be back home for a while and out of that trailer."

"I'm sure he is, though he doesn't mind traveling."

"Do you?"

"Mind traveling?"

"Yes. I would think it would grow old after a while."

He snorted a laugh and dug the toe of his boot into the dirt, holding the phone to his ear. "Wouldn't know what to do with myself if I wasn't on the road."

"Don't you have any hobbies?"

He thought about that for a minute, then shrugged. "Not that I can think of."

"Surely there's something you enjoy doing, besides wrestling steers?"

He chuckled and looked up at the moon again, propping an elbow on the arm he folded across his chest, enjoying the sound of her voice after two full days without having that small pleasure. "Nope. Too busy chasing rodeos to do much else. What about you? What do you do when you aren't playing shopkeeper?"

"Lots of things. I read, do needlework, do a little gardening. I enjoy cook—" She stopped suddenly, without finishing the sentence. "Oh, my," she said, sounding embarrassed. "I never realized my life was so boring."

"Do you enjoy doing those things you mentioned?" he asked.

"Well, yes," she said, her surprise obvious. "Of course I do."

"Then I guess you don't find them boring."

"Well, no. I don't. But in comparison to yours, my life must seem awfully dull."

"Dull?" He chuckled, shaking his head. "I don't recall a dull moment the entire time I was with you. And you forgot to add gambling to your list," he reminded her. "You're a damn good gambler."

She laughed softly, the sound warming Troy all the way to his toes. "Beginner's luck."

"I think you might have sent some of that luck my way," Troy said, smiling, too. "I've won money in every rodeo I've entered since I met you."

"Well, if I did, I'm glad. You certainly deserve it, after all you've done for me."

Troy's smile slowly wilted, the gratitude in her voice reminding him of their arrangement. "Shelby?"

"Yes?"

"You never said much about the baby's father."

There was a pause filled with such silence Troy could hear the thunder of his own heart beating in his ears.

"There's really nothing to tell."

Irritated by her answer, but not sure why, he snapped, "I'd think there would be. You're carrying his baby."

As soon as the callous words were out of his mouth, he wanted to snatch them back. He raked a hand through his hair. "I'm sorry, Shelby. I had no right to say that."

"Yes you did," she replied, but he could hear the hurt in her voice. "You have every right to ask about him. After all, you've given his baby your name. Something he wasn't willing to do." She took a deep breath, one in which he thought he heard a tremble before she spoke again.

"His name is Derrick Dominick and he lives in Denver. I met him there at an antique sale a little over six months ago. He's a collector. We had an affair."

"You don't have to tell me this," Troy said, feeling as low as a snake for making her feel as if she had to share with him what must be painful memories.

"Yes, I believe I do," she replied. He heard the resentment in her voice, as well as the determination. "The affair lasted a little over four months, with us being…intimate only three times. Though we used contraceptives, I became pregnant. You know the rest of the story."

Three times over a four-month period? Troy found it hard to believe that two people in love couldn't find the time to see each other more frequently than that. "Do you love him?"

Troy didn't know where the question came from, or even why he asked it. He just knew that he dreaded like hell hearing her answer.

"Whether I love him or not doesn't matter," she replied tersely. "The fact is, I'm pregnant with his child and he wants nothing to do with me or our baby." She sighed then, her weariness with the subject obvious. "I'm really tired, Troy. I think we had better say good-night."

"But, Shelby—"

"Good night, Troy."

Before he could apologize further, there was a click and a dial tone. He held the phone to his ear a moment longer, then, swearing, reared back and threw it as far as he could.

Five

It took Troy over an hour to find the phone in the darkness.
The only thing that kept him searching through the tall
grass was knowing that the cell phone was Shelby's only
means of contacting him…and he knew he wouldn't call
her again. Not after she'd hung up on him.

Furious with himself for pressing her for answers about
the man she'd had an affair with, he strode to his truck,
fished a sleeping bag from behind the seat, then headed for
the barn and the hayloft, opting to sleep there rather than
suffer the memories he'd find in the house.

It took a while for him to calm down enough to sleep.
But even then he wasn't able to rest fully, his dreams of
Shelby making that impossible. The content of the dreams
varied, but all ended the same, with him reaching for
Shelby, almost having a hand on her, then her slipping from
his grasp and disappearing into a vaporous cloud.

But then a new set of images slipped into his subconscious mind, these more familiar, darker, drawing him back into a time he wanted desperately to forget.

"Mama?" The little boy poked at his mother's shoulder. *"Mama, I don't feel so good."*

When his mother didn't respond, he crawled across the seat of the car and knelt beside her, placing a small hand on her shoulder. "Mama!" he said more loudly, then gulped, trying to swallow back the nausea that rose. He gave her a hard shake. "Mama, I'm gonna throw up!"

His mother's bent head lolled to the side, her eyes closed, her mouth slack. Her hand slipped lifelessly from the steering wheel to fall onto the seat, bumping against his scraped knee. But still she didn't respond. Feeling the bile rising higher, tearfully the boy scooted back across the seat and reached for the door handle. With a last furtive glance over his shoulder at his mother, he opened the door and slipped from the car, closing the door behind him.

He stumbled five steps, hoping to make it back to the house or at least to the barn, then sank to his hands and knees, retching, hanging his throbbing head between his braced arms while he emptied his stomach onto the dry grass.

The images fast-forwarded as the sleeping Troy thrashed in the sweat-soaked sleeping bag, trying to escape the nightmare.

"Troy!"

The little boy curled into a tighter ball in the hayloft, trembling at the sound of the angry voice.

"Troy!"

Squeezing his eyes shut, the little boy wedged himself deeper between the bales of hay, silent tears rolling down his cheeks.

A hand closed over his slim shoulder, the blunt fingers digging deep, and hauled him from his hiding place.

"Where's your mother?"

"I...I don't know," the little boy lied, *shrinking away from his grandfather.*

A hand shot out, the wide palm striking the little boy hard across the face and making his ears ring. Sobbing, the boy strained against the hand that held him.

"Where is she!" his grandfather demanded angrily, giving him a hard shake.

Knowing that refusing to answer was useless, the boy dropped his chin against his chest in defeat. "In...in the car. Out by the creek," he added, crying brokenly.

Snarling, his grandfather dragged him from the loft and out into the sunshine, his steps long and angry as he marched for the creek, towing the whimpering boy behind him.

The man lifted his head as he approached the car, hearing the sound of the engine running. "What the hell does she think she's doing letting the car idle like that and wasting my good gas!" His fingers bit deeper into the little boy's arm. "Probably listening to that damn trashy music. Well, she'll pay, dammit. That whoring daughter of mine will pay this time."

When he reached the car, he yanked open the door on the driver's side, then fell back a step, swearing, when the woman slumped behind the wheel slid lifelessly to the ground at his feet.

The little boy screamed, trying to tug free of his grandfather's grasp. Sobbing, he reached for her. "Ma-a-a-m-a-a!"

Troy jackknifed to a sitting position, his chest heaving, sweat pouring down his face. Groaning, he covered his face with his hands. Would it never end? Would he never escape the nightmares, the guilt? He inhaled deeply, once, twice, then slowly dragged his hands down his face to stare at the loft's window.

Sunshine poured through the opening, dust motes dancing in the beam of light.

He hadn't been able to help his mother, he told himself, scowling, but by God he could help Shelby.

Setting his jaw, he rose, grabbing up the sleeping bag and wadding it into a ball as he climbed down the loft's ladder. He cursed himself for a fool as he packed his gear and loaded Danny Boy into the trailer.

Why'd he have to go prying into Shelby's past? Why had he asked her if she loved the man? Why, for God's sake, had he even dialed her number in the first place? Why hadn't he simply waited for her to call him, as planned?

Not wanting to examine the reasons too closely, he climbed into his truck and slammed the door. He reached for the key and turned the ignition, then quickly shut it off. Pressing a shoulder against the door, he opened it and dropped to the ground, loping across the lawn to the house. When he stepped out onto the porch again, he carried a garment bag holding what his grandmother had always referred to as his Sunday-go-to-meeting clothes. He supposed they'd do for a wedding.

That is, if Shelby ever called to tell him the time and date.

Shelby sighed wearily as she climbed the stairs to her apartment, still reeling from her father's visit. Sunday right after church, he'd said. Pressing a hand to her aching forehead, she opened the door to her apartment and collapsed onto the sofa. Toeing off her shoes, she lifted her swollen feet to the trunk, propping them there, while she laid her head back and closed her eyes.

Almost a week had passed without a sign of her father or a word from him. Not that she'd expected him to call or drop by. Silence was a punishment that he used frequently when he was angry with her.

She sighed again, knowing that she had to call Troy and give him the news.

But she didn't want to call Troy. Not after their last conversation. His questions had left her feeling foolish and more than a little depressed.

Oh, what he must think of her! she cried silently. Giving herself so freely to a man as shallow as Derrick Dominick. Any fool should have been able to see beyond Derrick's handsome and polished exterior to the cold and selfish man within. But not Shelby Cannon, the innocent and overprotected preacher's daughter! She'd plunged blindly into the affair, sure that she'd found the man of her dreams, a man who her parents would approve and be proud of. But she'd quickly discovered, too late, that she'd been nothing to Derrick but a challenge. Another conquest. Another notch for his playboy belt.

But if she didn't call Troy, then she would have to lie to her father again, telling him that Troy couldn't make it back to Dunning for the wedding, that thirty-six hours was simply not enough notice for him to make the trip. And she could well imagine how her father would react to that news!

She sat up, her eyes going wide, as an idea occurred to her. But maybe Troy really couldn't make it to the wedding! He'd told her how harried his schedule was. How he raced from one rodeo to the next, with hardly time to even sleep. For all she knew, he could be in Timbuktu, and unable to make it back to Dunning in time for the wedding. She might not have to lie, after all!

She glanced at her wristwatch, wondering where Troy would be at six o'clock on a Friday evening and wondering, too, if he'd have his cellular phone with him, wherever he was. Slipping the fuel invoice from her skirt pocket, she leaned to pick up the portable phone from its base on the end table. After punching in his number, she waited, holding her breath, for the first ring.

When it came, it was broken off before it could fully sound, and Troy's voice came through. "Hello? Shelby? Is that you?"

Surprised by the panic in his voice, and even more so that he would assume she was calling, Shelby sank back against the sofa's cushions. "Y-yes. It's me."

"Are you all right? Nothing's happened has it? I mean, there isn't anything wrong with you or the baby, is there?"

She blinked back tears, touched by the concern in his voice, not only for her, but for her baby. Once again she found herself wishing that she'd fallen for a man like Troy, instead of a heartless man as Derrick had proven to be. "No. I'm fine. We both are," she said, laying a hand over the gentle swell of her stomach.

His sigh of relief was audible. "Thank God. I haven't heard from you since…well, since last week when we talked, and I thought for sure your daddy would have set a date and time by now. When you didn't call, I thought something must have happened, or—" Unwilling to admit that he'd feared that she would never call back, he cut himself off short and said instead, "I'm glad y'all are all right."

"There's no need to worry about us, Troy," she said softly. "My family's here. If something were to happen, I'd call them."

"Oh."

Hearing the disappointment in his voice and touched by it, she added, "But I appreciate your concern. I really do."

"Well, if you need anything—*anything*," he repeated adamantly, "all you have to do is call. I can be there in a matter of hours."

"Where are you, anyway?" she asked.

"Kansas. But I'll be leaving here later tonight and heading for Oklahoma. There's a rodeo at the Lazy E in Guthrie. I promised Yuma—he's a buddy of mine. I don't think I've mentioned him before. He's a steer wrestler, too. Anyway," he went on, aware that he was running at the mouth but unable to stop, fearing if he did, she'd hang up, "I promised Yuma I'd haze for him, then I entered up, too, figuring I best ride this lucky streak as long as I can."

"Haze?" she repeated, obviously unfamiliar with the term.

"Yeah. Haze," he said and tried to think how best to explain what that entailed. "See, you need another rider on the opposite side of the steer to keep the steer running straight, so you can pen the animal between you. Otherwise, once the chute opens, the steer could just take off running across the arena, and the cowboy would never have a chance to make his leap and take him down."

"Oh," she said slowly. "That makes sense...I guess."

"Probably would make better sense if you could see it. I'm not too good with words."

"You are wonderful with words," she scolded gently. "Don't be ridiculous."

There was a small pause, then Troy asked hesitantly, "Shelby? Why'd you call?"

"Oh," she murmured, feeling her stomach knotting again. "Daddy came by this afternoon and said he wants to perform the ceremony on Sunday right after church."

"This Sunday?"

She heard the hesitancy in his voice and was sure he was trying to think of a way to weasel out of the obligation. "But don't feel as if you have to change your schedule," she hastened to assure him. "I'll just tell Daddy that you already had plans for that day and they couldn't be changed."

"I can make it."

"That isn't necessary, Troy," she lectured sternly. "You'll be in Oklahoma Saturday night. There's no way you can make it to Dunning in time for a wedding on Sunday."

"Sure there is," he told her. "What time is the church service over?"

"About noon. Unless daddy gets really wound up. When he does, his sermons tend to run a little long."

"Yeah," he said dryly. "I can just imagine."

Shelby started to laugh, but quickly swallowed the laughter, thinking of the physical strain placed on Troy if he tried to make the trip. "Really, Troy," she urged, "you don't have to do this."

"I know I don't. But I want to."

Bleary-eyed from lack of sleep, and all but drunk from staring at a white line for eleven hours, Tory forced his eyes wider, trying to keep the highway in focus.

"Just another couple of miles," he promised himself, "and you're home free."

Well, not free exactly, he thought glancing nervously at the clock on the dash. Unless, of course, this was one of those Sundays when Shelby's father got himself all stirred up preaching the gospel, and the church service ran past noon. If so, then he might not be showing up an hour late for his own wedding. He might be right on time.

But if the man wasn't preaching long, Troy feared he'd have hell to pay. And the first payment due would be to the preacher.

Scowling, he pressed the accelerator a little closer to the floorboard and took the Dunning exit, squealing tires. Minutes later he pulled up in front of the church, noting with relief that the parking lot was still full. He shot another glance at the clock on the dash and decided to hell with the suit hanging behind him; there simply wasn't time to change.

Leaping from his truck, he raced down the sidewalk and up the steps, sure that he would find a church full of people all shaking their heads and whispering about poor little Shelby being left at the altar by that no-good cowboy. Another black mark against the Cannons' already tarnished name.

Hoping to spare Shelby any more humiliation than she'd already suffered because of him, he burst through the vestibule doors with enough force to make them slam back against the sanctuary walls. He stopped short, his chest heaving, as every head in the church turned to stare at him, eyes wide in shock. Beyond them, he saw Reverend Cannon on the raised dais, decked out in full battle uniform—flowing black robe and stiff white collar—his fist poised in midair, caught just short of pounding the pulpit by Troy's explosive entrance.

The whole scene looked to Troy like something out of a B movie. And that was before he considered his own sorry state.

Boots scarred and dusty, their soles still carrying dirt clods from the arena he'd competed in the night before. A brand of that same dirt staining the seat of his jeans and one elbow where he'd sat down hard while throwing the steer he'd drawn. The sweat-stained hat he wore on his head, which might, if he was lucky, be hiding his bloodshot eyes and shadowing a day's growth of beard.

Remembering his manners, he dragged off the hat and glanced slowly around the hushed church, swallowing the apology he'd been ready to offer for being late. His eyes settled on Shelby, seated at the front row. She rose as his gaze met hers, and started toward him, her forehead creased in concern.

The dress she wore was simple, the color of weak tea,

and cut full, like every other outfit she wore, to conceal the slight swell of her stomach. No white for this pregnant bride, he thought with regret.

As she neared, she reached out and caught his free hand in hers. "Troy? Are you all right?"

Swallowing hard, he tore his gaze from hers and glanced behind her at the parishioners, who still gaped at him, their faces all mirroring the same shocked expression. Beyond them Reverend Cannon stood, his fist still poised in the air. The music director took a step forward from the choir loft and pulled his reading glasses down on his nose to peer at Troy over the top, his mouth pursed in disapproval.

"That's him!" he heard a warbled voice cry in a loud whisper. "That's the man who claimed to be Shelby's husband."

He shifted his gaze to the third row on the right and saw Maybelle Porter sitting with her gray head tipped to her neighbor's ear.

Shelby squeezed his hand, drawing his gaze back to hers. "Is something wrong?"

Unable to speak, he shook his head. "I…I thought I was late," he said, finding his voice. "The rodeo ran long, and I wasn't able to leave as soon as I'd hoped. You said to be here by twelve. It's almost one."

She shook her head, the creases on her forehead deepening. "But it's not quite noon. The church service isn't even over yet."

Groaning, Troy closed his eyes and dropped his chin to his chest. "The time change," he muttered miserably, his fingers going limp in hers. "I forgot about the time change." Sighing, he lifted his head and looked across the church at her father.

If looks could kill, Troy knew he'd be a dead man. Knowing there was nothing for him to do but try and make the best of an already bad situation, he tipped his head in greeting. "Sorry, Reverend. I thought I was late to the wedding."

The man's chest swelled beneath his robe, and his lips thinned in anger. "If it's all right with you," he said tersely, "I'd like to finish my sermon."

Troy gave his chin a jerk and slipped onto an empty seat on the last pew, tugging Shelby down beside him. Inhaling deeply, he pulled their still-joined hands to rest on his thigh, then released the breath on a long sigh when the preacher cleared his throat and resumed his sermon.

If there had been a test afterward, Troy would have failed it, not having heard a word the preacher said. All he could think about was the warmth of Shelby's hand in his, the comfort, the pressure of her slim shoulder resting against his arm, the scent of roses that swirled around him, filling his senses. He stole a glance at her during the benediction, when he should have had his head bowed and his eyes closed, and found her looking at him. The sweetness of her expression, the intensity with which she was studying him caught his breath, and a pain like nothing he'd experienced in his life tore through his chest.

God help him…he was falling in love with her.

"By the power vested in me by God, the church and the state of New Mexico, I now pronounce you husband and wife." Frowning, the preacher waved an impatient hand at Troy and added grudgingly, "You may kiss the bride."

With his gaze fixed on Shelby's, Troy hesitated, unsure if he should take advantage of the gift the preacher offered him, knowing he had no right, no matter how many powers the preacher had vested in him. Shelby wasn't his wife. Not really. Not even with the promises he'd made to love and keep her until death do them part still echoing in his mind. And he would cut off his arm before he'd do anything that would cause her discomfort or embarrassment.

But while he was vacillating, her hands gripped tightly in his, she rose to her toes and lifted her face expectantly to his. With his heart pounding in his ears, he bent his head over hers, intending to brush her lips with his, keeping the kiss as chaste as possible. But when his mouth met hers and he got that first taste of her, he crumbled at the sweetness, the innocence he discovered there. Dropping her hands, he wrapped his arms around her and drew her into the circle of his embrace, lengthening the kiss, then taking it deeper.

The feeling that swept over him was much like that which he'd experienced the first time he'd made the leap from a horse's back to wrestle a steer to the ground. That sense of time stopping, of everything slipping into slow motion, his heart hammering a hole in his chest, his blood racing like something wild through his veins. The temporary sense of weightlessness while falling, yet knowing that he was bound to hit the ground hard soon.

He wasn't sure how long the kiss lasted, but he slowly became aware of laughter, a scattering of applause. Remembering the parishioners who had stayed to witness their vows, he dragged his mouth from Shelby's and withdrew far enough to meet her gaze, his chest heaving, his lungs burning. The eyes that met his were luminous, startled...and filled with enough heat that it was all he could do to keep from pulling her into his arms once more and claiming her mouth with his again.

Mrs. Cannon had baked a wedding cake and made a huge bowl of punch, which she served in the church parlor to those who had stayed to witness their vows. Troy stood beside Shelby at the door, shaking hands with the guests as they filed by and offering vague answers to the questions of those bold enough to ask.

He heaved a sigh of relief when the last guest moved past him to visit with Shelby's mother.

"I'll be right back," Shelby whispered. "I'm going to the ladies' room."

Troy nodded absently as he worked a finger behind the tie he'd donned before the ceremony, along with his Sunday-go-to-meeting clothes. Craning his neck, he tugged, trying to give himself some breathing room.

"Well, I don't know," he heard Mrs. Cannon say hesitantly. "Troy?"

He glanced her way. "Yes, ma'am?"

"Will you be making your home in Dunning?"

"Oh, no, ma'am. I've got a place in Texas." Seeing the look of alarm that widened her eyes, he realized too late that she must think he was taking her daughter away from her and moving her off to Texas. Hoping to reassure her, he added quickly, "But Shelby will be staying on here."

He stifled a groan at the number of eyebrows that shot up at his reply. Wondering how he'd managed to wedge a size-thirteen boot so soundly in his mouth, he tried to smooth over the slip. "You see, I'm on the road most of the time, so it doesn't make much sense for Shelby to move to Texas. She'd be alone most of the time, whereas she'll have y'all nearby if she stays here in Dunning."

"On the road?"

Troy shifted his gaze to the woman who'd started all the ruckus when she'd asked Shelby's mother where he and Shelby were planning to live.

"Yes, ma'am. I'm a professional cowboy and travel the rodeo circuit, so I'm gone more than I'm home."

"Really?" the woman said, her interest obvious. "I have a nephew who's a bull rider. He competes on the college level."

"That's a good place to get some experience," Troy offered, relieved to have the focus of the conversation shift away from him. "It'll prepare him for the pros, if he should decide to make a career of rodeoing."

"My husband and I are big rodeo fans. Go every chance we get. Will you be competing near here anytime soon?"

"Not for a while," he told the woman. "I'll be leaving this afternoon for the rodeo in Durango. Then I'll be going home to Texas for a few days to catch up on some work there."

"Will Shelby be going with you?"

"Going where?" Shelby asked, smiling, as she rejoined them.

"With Troy," the woman said. "He was just telling us that he's leaving this afternoon for a rodeo in Durango, then going home to Texas for a few days."

Shelby looked up at Troy, her smile melting, her eyes filled with panic, obviously not having given any thought to what would occur once they'd repeated their vows. "W-well, no," she stammered.

"Of course you're going with him," her mother said in dismay. "You're newlyweds!"

"But I have the shop to run," Shelby argued, grasping at any reasonable excuse. "I can't just close it up for a week."

"Pooh," her mother said, dismissing her daughter's argument with a wave of her hand. "I can mind the shop. I've done it before. Besides, a woman's place is with her husband. Isn't that right, Troy?"

Troy glanced at Shelby, trying to get a feel for what she wanted him to say. When he couldn't, he answered with what was in his heart.

"Yes, ma'am. Shelby belongs with me."

After an hour of driving in a strained silence, Troy glanced Shelby's way and found her face still turned to the passenger window, her arms crossed underneath her breasts.

"I can take you back home, if you want," he offered quietly.

Sighing, she turned from the window and dipped her chin to her chest as she smoothed the wrinkles from the skirt of her dress. "No," she said miserably. "That would just give the citizens of Dunning more to talk about." She turned to look at him, her eyes filled with regret. "I'm so sorry, Troy."

"For what?" he asked in confusion, sure that he was the one who owed the apology for putting her in a position where she had no choice but to leave with him.

"After all you've done, and now you're stuck with me for a whole week."

Stuck with her? He would have laughed at the irony in the statement if she hadn't looked so serious. Turning his gaze back to the windshield, he lifted a shoulder. "I don't consider myself stuck, at all. In fact, I'm glad for the company. Traveling alone gets mighty lonesome."

"Still..."

He arched a brow and glanced her way. "I imagine we could argue this another hundred miles or so, or we could both just agree to make the best of the hand we've been dealt. For my part, I plan on enjoying your company. What about you?"

She stared at him a moment, as if unsure of her response, then squared her shoulders and gave her chin a purposeful lift. "I plan to enjoy."

"Atta girl," he said, and shot her a wink.

He'd expected a smile from her, or at least a relaxing of her tensed shoulders, but the worry lines remained on her forehead and even deepened a bit as she caught her lower lip between her teeth.

"Is there something else bothering you?" he asked cautiously.

"No," she said slowly. "Not really. But I do think it's important for you to know that I will stay out of your way, that I won't intrude upon your…upon your…"

"Upon my what?" he asked, frowning, when she hesitated.

"Your intimate life," she said in a rush, then spun to face the window again, her cheeks flaming.

It took Troy a minute to figure out what she was talking about. When he did, he had to work hard to keep from laughing. He feared if he did laugh, though, he would only embarrass her more. "If you're concerned about any women in my life, there's no need to worry, because there aren't any."

She glanced over her shoulder. "None?"

Though he had managed not to laugh, he couldn't suppress the smile that her startled expression drew. "No, ma'am. The only people who would be affected by you traveling with me are Pete and Clayton, and that's only because they'd have to watch their manners with a woman along."

"Will they be joining us?"

"No." He chuckled when he saw her shoulders relax, thankful, for her sake, that his traveling buddies weren't along on this trip. He had a feeling that Shelby's sheltered upbringing wouldn't have prepared her for the shock of living out of a truck with three rowdy men. "Pete's at Clayton's ranch," he explained, "taking care of things while Clayton's in Oklahoma trying to talk his wife into coming back home. So it'll be just you and me and Danny Boy making the trip to the Durango rodeo." He cut a glance her way. "Ever been to the Durango rodeo?"

"I've never been to *any* rodeo," she admitted sheepishly.

His eyes widened in dismay. "Hell, that's almost un-American!"

She laughed and shifted on the seat, angling her body toward him, seemingly more at ease. "It wasn't that I didn't want to. Daddy just didn't—well, I think you can imagine his reasons."

"I take it he keeps a pretty short leash on you, huh?"

"Yes, but I guess that's understandable, considering the trouble my sister managed to get herself into."

"Trouble that he's making you pay for," he reminded her, unable to keep the resentment from his voice.

"No," she replied, shaking her head in disagreement. "I've never felt as if he was punishing me for her mistakes. Certainly not then, and I don't believe he is now, either. At least, not intentionally. He just wants to protect me. I think he felt responsible for my sister's actions, as if he could have prevented what happened if he had intervened and forbidden her to see Marshall, the man she ran away with."

"Nobody can stop a person from doing something, if that person wants to do it badly enough."

"Maybe," she said slowly. "But I don't blame my father for trying to protect me," she added. "He has his faults, but I've never doubted his love for me."

If possible, Shelby's comment made Troy's admiration for her grow another notch or two. He couldn't think of many people who would share her feelings if similarly treated.

"How long ago did all this happen?" he asked curiously.

"About ten years ago. I was thirteen, and my sister had just turned nineteen."

"Are y'all still in contact with her?"

"Heavens, no!" she exclaimed. "Though the fault for that is hers, not my family's," she added. "Daddy hired a private investigator to find her, then went to Dallas to try to persuade her to come home. But she refused. She and Marshall had married by then and had spent most of the funds she had stolen from the church.''

"How did she manage to get off the hook? Seems the law would have stepped in and demanded restitution?''

"I honestly don't know the details, but I think it was because the money belonged to the church. Daddy met with the officials of the church, as well as the deacons, and told them the whole story, promising to repay every cent that was missing if they would agree not to press charges. He even paid for the audit that was ordered on the church's books.''

"With your college money.''

"Yes, but please don't think I hold any ill feelings that he did. I don't. The money was never mine. It was saved by my parents and was theirs to spend as they saw fit. They did what they felt they had to do...what was best for the family.''

Troy glanced her way, unable to believe that anyone could have a heart as pure, as unselfish, as Shelby seemed to have. He turned to stare at the windshield, wondering again how a woman like her had ever become involved with a man low enough to refuse to acknowledge a child he'd bred, a man who would leave a woman like Shelby to deal with the pregnancy alone.

"Troy?''

"Hmm?'' he murmured absently.

"I did love him,'' she said quietly.

He snapped his head around. "Who?'' he asked uneasily, sure that she'd read his thoughts.

"Derrick.'' She dropped her gaze. "Or, at least, I thought I did. Now I'm not so sure.'' She caught her bottom lip between her teeth and plucked at the fabric on her skirt. "I'm really sorry that I was so rude to you that night on the phone when you asked me about him.''

"You don't have to apologize. I had no right to pry into your private life."

"But you do have a right," she insisted, lifting her gaze to his. "You are entitled to know everything about the man whose baby will carry your name."

"He's not the baby's father," Troy said angrily, surprised by the level of resentment he felt. "Not in the way that counts most."

"I suppose you're right." She drew in a shuddery breath as she turned to stare at the windshield, unable to meet his gaze any longer. "I don't want you to think that I—well, that I'm the type of woman who gives herself freely to a man."

"I never thought that," he said gruffly, hearing the shame in her voice, "though I did question your judgment in the man you chose to keep company with."

She almost smiled at the old-fashioned phrase he used to describe her affair. Almost. But the pain returned, the shame. "I've questioned that, too," she admitted reluctantly. "I've had a lot of time to think about my relationship with Derrick, and I'm not very proud of the discoveries I've made about myself."

"We all make mistakes. I'm sure even your daddy has made a few."

She smiled then, and glanced his way. "None that he would ever admit."

He snorted. "Probably not. But he's human. Trust me. He's made his fair share."

She sighed again and dipped her chin, smoothing her hands over the dress of her skirt. "It shames me to admit it, but the fault for the affair is mine."

"It takes two," he reminded her.

"Yes, but upon reflection, I can see that I was ready for an affair. Curious even. Heavens! I was twenty-three years old, a virgin, and with very little experience with men. I wanted desperately to fall in love, to marry, to have a husband that my family could be proud of, a family of my own.''

Troy wanted to tell her he didn't need to hear these things, had no desire to know the intimate details of her relationship with the man she'd slept with, the man who had fathered the baby she carried. But he sensed that she needed to talk, and it seemed he was the only one around to listen.

''Derrick was handsome,'' she said thoughtfully, as if thinking out loud. ''Intelligent, attentive. And passionate,'' she added, and blushed slightly. ''Meeting him and being with him was the most exciting thing that had ever happened to me. When we were apart, all I did was think about him, dream about him, plan ways to be able to see him again. I lived for his phone calls. Would lie awake at night and replay our conversations, analyzing every word, every sigh. And when we were together...''

She stopped and dipped her chin again, obviously embarrassed. ''Well, our relationship progressed quickly to a physical one. I was madly in love with him, and was sure that he shared my feelings. When I discovered that I was pregnant, I was terrified, yet secretly thrilled, thinking that Derrick would be excited, too, once he got over the initial shock, and that we would marry.''

She lifted her face to stare through the windshield, though he was sure she saw none of the landscape they passed. ''Discovering that he wasn't excited, that he wanted nothing to do with me or our baby, was a horrific blow. Brutal. Humiliating. Frightening, when I discovered that I was in this alone.''

Out of the corner of his eye, Troy watched a shudder move through her and could only imagine how devastating that last confrontation must have been for her.

''You're better off without him,'' he said gruffly, wishing he could have five minutes alone with the man who had done this to her. He would make this Derrick guy think twice before he seduced another innocent woman into his bed.

"Yes," she murmured. "And wiser, too. Much wiser." She felt a hand close over hers and glanced down, then up at him in surprise.

"Some kinds of education come harder than others," he told her quietly, his gray eyes warm on hers. He turned to face the road again and gave her hand a reassuring squeeze. "But don't beat yourself up for trusting a man who didn't deserve it in the first place. He's the fool. Not you."

GET FREE BOOKS and a FREE GIFT
WHEN YOU PLAY THE...

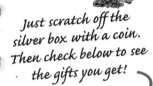

Lucky 7

SLOT MACHINE GAME!

Just scratch off the silver box with a coin. Then check below to see the gifts you get!

YES! I have scratched off the silver box. Please send me the 2 free books and gift for which I qualify. I understand I am under no obligation to purchase any books, as explained on the back of this card.

326 SDL C4GV

225 SDL C4GR
(S-D-OS-08/00)

NAME   (PLEASE PRINT CLEARLY)

ADDRESS

APT.#   CITY

STATE/PROV.   ZIP/POSTAL CODE

7	7	7	**Worth TWO FREE BOOKS plus a BONUS Mystery Gift!**
🍒	🍒	🍒	**Worth TWO FREE BOOKS!**
♣	♣	♣	**Worth ONE FREE BOOK!**
🔔	🔔	🍒	**TRY AGAIN!**

DETACH AND MAIL CARD TODAY!

Six

The rodeo grounds were dark when they arrived, with only a few security lights to guide their way as Troy steered his truck to the long row of metal buildings that housed the stalls. Trucks of various sizes and descriptions were scattered around the parking area, most of which were hooked to empty horse trailers. Men stood in loose groups, talking and laughing. A few raised a hand in greeting as they drove by, obviously recognizing Troy's truck.

After pulling up alongside one of the buildings, Troy set the brake and opened his door. "I'll unload Danny Boy and settle him in a stall, then we'll find us a place to stay for the night."

Yawning wearily, Shelby nodded, then climbed from the truck, relieved that their journey was nearing an end. She walked to the rear of the trailer and stood off to the side, stretching her aching back as she watched Troy unload the horse.

"Want to walk with us, while Danny Boy gets the kinks out?" he asked as he backed the horse from the trailer.

"Sure." She fell into step beside him, but had to quickly increase her pace to match his longer stride.

"Sorry," he said, reducing the length of his step to accommodate hers. "I forget how short your legs are."

"My legs aren't short," she replied indignantly. "*Yours* are just too long."

Troy stopped to open a gate and shot her a teasing grin. "If you say so…shorty." Chuckling when she pursed her lips, frowning at him, he led the horse inside. "Wait here," he instructed and closed the gate, locking her on the outside. "I'm gonna let him run a minute."

Careful to watch where she stepped, Shelby eased to the side of the round pen and peered through the slats, watching as Troy moved to the center of the small space. He fed out the lead rope until half the diameter of the pen separated him from the horse, then clicked his tongue once, and Danny Boy stepped off into a trot along the wall, his head high, his mane flying.

Troy turned in a tight circle, guiding the horse round and round, then clicked again and the horse broke into a canter. Though the sight of the powerful animal moving in the soft golden glow from the security light was breathtaking, Shelby found her gaze straying again and again to Troy.

Rugged, masculine, strong. There were a dozen adjectives that she could think of to describe him, but not a one of them gave justice to the man she'd come to know. He was kind and gentle and considerate, traits that the casual observer might miss but that Shelby knew were there because she'd witnessed them all firsthand.

"Well, howdy, ma'am!"

Startled by the deep, male voice, she whirled to find a man striding up behind her. She couldn't make out his features in the darkness, but she could see that he was as tall as Troy…and probably about thirty pounds heavier. His size alone was enough to intimidate her, and she took a nervous step back.

"H-hello," she returned uneasily.

He nodded his head toward the round pen. "That's some mighty bad company you're keepin'."

"Leave the lady alone," Troy called from inside the round pen. "She's with me."

"That's exactly my point," the cowboy replied. "And as a gentleman, I feel it's my moral duty to rescue her 'fore she ruins her reputation hangin' out with the likes of you."

Not certain whether the man was safe or not, Shelby eased her spine against the metal rails of the round pen, unsure whether she should make a run for the truck or try to scale the fence and hide behind Troy. Before she could decide which option to take, the gate squeaked open beside her and Troy stepped through, leading Danny Boy.

"If you're a gentleman," Troy said dryly, "then I'm the president of the United States."

"Which would give me even more cause to rescue the lady from you." Laughing, the cowboy slapped Troy on the back. "Was wonderin' if you were gonna make it back in time."

"I told you I'd be here."

"That you did," the cowboy agreed amiably. He reared back and looked at Shelby again. "Well, are you gonna introduce me to this little lady, or not?"

Troy glanced toward Shelby. "Shelby, this is Yuma, one of the poorest excuses for a steer wrestler you'll ever meet. Yuma, this is my wife, Shelby."

The tag "my wife" was out of Troy's mouth before he realized that it probably wasn't necessary to continue the charade outside of Dunning. But it was too late now. Yuma let out a whoop loud enough to make a deaf man wince.

"Wife! You mean this sweet little thang was fool enough to marry an old coot like you?"

"Yeah," Troy said, shooting Shelby an apologetic look.

"Hey, boys!" Yuma yelled over his shoulder. "Troy's gotten himself married! Come on over here and meet his new bride."

Troy dumped his duffel bag on the floor, then tossed Shelby's suitcase onto the bed with a heavy sigh. "Damn, I'm sorry, Shelby," he muttered, dragging off his hat. "But I couldn't very well request two rooms, not with Yuma and all the guys standing there looking on." He raked a hand through his hair, combing the dark strands into stiff spikes. "I never dreamed that they'd be staying here, too. They usually bunk up in their trailers at the rodeo arena. It was just bad timing that they walked into the lobby just as I was about to request two rooms."

"It's okay," she assured him for at least the third time since they'd left the registration desk. "Really. I know it couldn't be helped."

"I'll sleep on the floor," he offered, and opened the closet's bifold doors in search of a blanket. "You can have the bed."

"Don't be ridiculous." She pushed his hand out of the way as he reached for the blanket on the top shelf and closed the doors with a snap. "We've shared a bed before without a problem. I'm sure we can do so again."

An hour later Shelby wondered if that was true. Though exhausted, she couldn't fall asleep. And it seemed Troy suffered the same malady. He'd flipped from his back to his stomach four times within the past ten minutes. Shelby knew because she had counted each turn.

"Troy?"

"Hmm?" he murmured from the other side of the king-size bed.

"Are you cool enough?"

"Yeah. Why?"

"I just wondered."

"Are you?"

"Yes, thank you. I'm fine."

She inhaled deeply, counted to ten, then slowly released the breath just as Troy flipped again, this time to his back.

"Troy?"

"What?"

"Are you uncomfortable sleeping with your jeans on?"

"Yeah, but that's okay."

She caught her lower lip between her teeth, knowing that he'd made the concession for her benefit. "You can take them off, if you like. I don't mind."

She felt the mattress shift as he lifted his head to peer at her in the darkness.

"You sure?" he asked uncertainly.

"Positive," she told him, and turned her head to offer him a confident smile.

"Well, if you're sure," he murmured as he slipped from beneath the covers and stood beside the bed.

When he reached for his zipper, Shelby snapped her head back around to stare at the ceiling again, swallowing hard. She heard the rasp of his zipper, then the soft whisper of denim sliding down his legs. Unable to resist, she stole a peek just as he lifted a bare foot to tug the jeans over his left heel. Though the room was dark, she could just make out his shape. His broad back, the muscles corded from his stooped position. The thick, elastic band of his underwear at his waist, the tapered hips that gave way to muscled thighs. The dark hair that shadowed his long legs.

Without meaning to, she did a quick mental comparison and discovered that Derrick came up short. Troy was much more muscular—a body type she found physically appealing—and yet another trait to add to the growing list of things she found appealing about Troy Jacobs.

As he turned back for the bed, she quickly faced the ceiling again, her cheeks hot, her heart racing. She felt the bed give beneath his weight as he lay back down with a sigh.

"Better?" she asked, trying to hide the tremble in her voice.

"Much. Thanks."

"Think you can sleep now?" she asked hopefully, knowing she didn't have a prayer of sleeping, as long as she knew he was awake.

"Yeah, I think so. How 'bout you?"

"I hope so."

"Need me to talk you to sleep again?"

She smiled at the teasing in his voice. "Thanks, but I think I can manage on my own this time."

She lay there wide-eyed, keenly aware of the man who lay beside her wearing nothing but his briefs, with a too-clear image of the muscular body beneath the sheet. Heat crawled through her body, knotting low in her belly, and her ears rang with the wild beating of her heart.

"Shelby?"

"Y-yes?"

"I really am sorry that I slipped up and introduced you as my wife."

"Don't be. I understand."

"To be honest, though, I don't know how I could have avoided it, without everybody thinking you were some buckle bunny."

She turned her face to peer at him. "Buckle bunny? What in the world is that?"

He chuckled and rolled to his side, facing her, his broad shoulders wide enough to block her view of the dresser behind him. "A girl who follows the rodeos, chasing after the cowboys. Some of 'em don't have the best of reputations, if you get my drift.''

In the darkness she could just make out his features. The high cheekbones, the nose with the slight hump along its ridge. The light scar that ran from the corner of his mouth and ended just below his cheek. His wasn't a pretty face, at least not in the commercial sense, but there was a ruggedness to his features, a strength, that she found unbelievably sexy.

And the grin he currently offered her, she found totally irresistible.

Smiling, she slipped a hand from beneath the covers and tapped a fingertip against the end of his nose. ''Then I guess I should thank you for saving my honor.''

Ducking his head back, he caught her hand in his, chuckling, then tucked her hand beneath his cheek as he laid his head back down on the pillow. ''You make me sound like some kind of white knight or something. A knight,'' he repeated, then snorted a disbelieving laugh. He nestled his cheek against the back of her hand, yawned hugely, then closed his eyes on a sigh.

Shelby watched him, listening as his heavy breathing grew rhythmic. He was a knight, she reflected wistfully, finding comfort in the scrape of his beard against her hand, warmth and a reassuring strength in the fingers wrapped around hers. He'd saved her family the disgrace associated with having an unwed pregnant daughter, and he'd saved her child the stigma of being born out of wedlock. Yes, he was a white knight, all right.

He was her white knight.

''You can watch from over there,'' Troy said, giving his chin a jerk toward the far corner of the arena. He gave the saddle's cinch a tug, tightening it around Danny Boy's middle, then dropped the stirrup from where he had hooked it over the saddle horn. "When it's time for the steer wrestlers to compete, we'll enter the arena from that gate there," he added, pointing, "and go to the far end, just to the left of the chute, where we'll wait our turns to compete. When we're all done, I'll meet you back here at the trailer."

Shelby nodded, wondering how he could sound so calm. Her own nerves were raw just thinking about him making that leap off Danny Boy's back, locking his arms around a horned steer and wrestling it to the ground.

Obviously sensing her fears, he laughed and slung an arm around her shoulders, guiding her away from the arena, leading his horse behind him. "What are you lookin' so scared about? It's me who's competing, not you."

She inhaled deeply and tried to relax her tensed shoulders beneath the weight of his arm. "Yes," she replied, ashamed of her cowardice. "Thankfully. I doubt I'd have the nerve to even climb on a horse, much less jump from one."

"Aww, come on now," he said, bumping a hip playfully against hers as they walked. "Give yourself some credit. I bet you'd get a kick out of grabbing a steer by the horns."

Shelby sputtered a laugh, then narrowed an eye at him. "Just be careful, okay? I don't want you hurt."

Chuckling, he hugged her against his side. "I won't get hurt. I promise."

"Well, would you look at that?" a voice called from behind them. "If it isn't Troy Jacobs all cuddled up with his new bride."

Shelby felt Troy stiffen, but he kept walking, tightening his hold on her while ignoring the man behind them.

"Where'd you find her, Troy?" the man called. "Steal her away from another man?"

Shelby could feel the rage vibrating through Troy and wondered who the man was and what the history was between them. And there was a history, she knew. She could tell by the anger she could feel swelling inside Troy.

"She looks awful sweet to be hooked up with a thieving scoundrel like you. Whadja do?" the man yelled. "Knock her up so she had no choice but to marry you?"

Troy swung around then, thrusting the reins into Shelby's hand. "Stay here," he ordered, his voice low and threatening.

"Troy, no," she said grabbing for him, sure that he meant to fight the man.

But he shrugged free of her grasp. "Stay," he repeated angrily.

He strode toward the man, his arms hanging stiffly out at his sides, looking like a gunfighter out of the Old West. The man who'd hurled the insult stood beside a horse trailer, one boot propped on the tire behind him, a toothpick dangling lazily from between his lips. As Troy neared, the man spat the toothpick out and straightened.

Troy stopped directly in front him. "You stay the hell away from my wife, Dakota," he warned darkly.

"And what are you going to do if I don't?" the man sneered. "Sic the law on me again?"

"No," Troy said, his voice deathly calm. "This time I'll beat the hell out of you myself."

The man swung, but Troy saw the punch coming and ducked, throwing up an arm to block the blow. Moving quickly, he caught Dakota's arm and twisted, spinning him around and pinning his arm behind his back. "Now I think you owe my wife an apology," he said through clenched teeth.

"I owe that whore of yours nothing," Dakota growled.

Troy spun him again, and slammed him up hard against the horse trailer. "Don't you *ever* call my wife that again," he said, thrusting his forearm harder against the man's neck. "Do you hear me?"

"Hey, Shelby! Where's Troy?"

Shelby whirled at the sound of Yuma's voice. "Oh,

Yuma,'' she cried, grabbing his arm. "You've got to stop them before someone is hurt!"

"Stop who?" Yuma asked, then swore, jerking free from her when he spotted Troy. "Kirby! Chico!" he called as he ran. "Get over here."

The two cowboys standing behind the chutes glanced over at the sound of their names, saw the problem and came at a run.

Yuma wrapped his arms around Troy's barrel-size chest from behind. "Come on, buddy," he said in a low voice. "He's not worth the busted knuckles. Let him go."

"Not until he apologizes to Shelby," Troy threatened, increasing the pressure on the man's neck.

Chico slipped up on one side of Dakota and Kirby the other, both bracing an elbow against the man's chest to hold him against the trailer as they tried to pry Troy's arm from his neck. But none of the men could break the hold Troy had on Dakota.

"Troy, please," Shelby cried from behind him. "It doesn't matter. Just let him go."

Troy thrust his arm harder against Dakota's throat, making the man's eyes bulge. "Say it," he ordered darkly. "Tell her you're sorry."

"S-s-sorry," the man gasped out, then bent double choking and gagging when Troy dropped his arm, releasing him.

"Don't let me catch you anywhere near her," he warned, "because if I do…" He let the threat hang unfinished, then turned and snatched the reins from Shelby's hand. Taking her by the arm, he muttered, "Come on. Let's get out of here."

Shelby had to almost run to keep up with his angry stride. "Who was that man?" she asked, peering up at Troy.

"Nobody," he muttered, his scowl darkening.

* * *

Shelby stood in the spot where Troy had left her, entrusted to Chico's care, waiting for the announcer to call Troy's name to compete. Her knees still shook from the fight she'd witnessed earlier.

She'd never seen Troy mad before. Angry, yes. But never mad. And she prayed she would never see him that way again.

But what concerned her the most was Troy's refusal to tell her who the man was, and what the fight was about.

"Chico?" she asked hesitantly.

"Yes?"

"Who was that man Troy was fighting with?"

"Dakota." He shook his head sadly. "He is one bad hombre, that Dakota."

"Have they had trouble before?"

Chico nodded, frowning, his gaze narrowed on the arena. "Many times. Dakota, he used to beat up on his wife. Especially when he'd been drinking. Troy heard her screaming one night and went to see what was wrong. Dakota had her on the ground and was beating her pretty bad. Took Troy and two other men to pull him off. Somebody called the cops, and Dakota spent a couple of weeks in jail, and his wife spent a couple of days in the hospital."

"But there were other men involved, plus the police," she said in dismay. "Yet Dakota seems to blame only Troy."

Chico cut a glance at her. "That's because Troy stayed involved." He sighed and turned his gaze back to the arena. "Troy visited her in the hospital, took her to his ranch and let her stay there while she was recuperating. Then he loaned her the money she needed to divorce Dakota and start over. Dakota, he's not a forgiving man."

"Were they...involved?" she asked hesitantly, unsure she wanted to hear his response.

Chico angled his head to frown at her. "Troy and Dakota's wife?"

At her slow nod, he snorted and shook his head. "No. There was never anything between them but Troy's desire to help the woman out of a bad situation."

Shelby curled her fingers around the rail of the fence and shifted her gaze to the arena and the group of riders huddled there. "He's a good man," she murmured.

"He's that and then some," Chico agreed with a jerk of his chin.

She frowned when she didn't see Troy in the group of men waiting to ride, and placed a sandal on the lowest rail, pulling herself up to peer over the top of the arena's fence. She finally spotted him, sitting astride Danny Boy on the far side of the group, Yuma at his side. She was disheartened to see that his jaw was still set in the same angry slash it had been when he'd left her.

A shiver chased down her spine as the scene replayed through her mind again. The growing tension in the hand Troy had held at her elbow while he'd ignored Dakota's heckling. The angry flush that had swept over his face when he'd spun to confront the man when Dakota had called Shelby a whore. The muscles that had corded on his back and neck as he'd held Dakota pinned against the side of the trailer.

Never in her life had anyone fought for her. And though it shamed her to admit it, she felt a small thrill of excitement, knowing that Troy cared enough to defend her honor.

But she'd also never known such a sickening fear.

What if the man had had a knife or a gun and had pulled it on Troy? Troy could have been killed trying to protect her. Stricken by the thought, she called out to him. "Troy!"

He glanced her way, frowning, then reined Danny Boy in her direction. "What?"

"I...I just wanted to wish you good luck," she said, and

forced a smile, hoping to tease some of the anger from him. "The proper thing to tell an actor about to go on the stage is 'break a leg.' What does one say to a cowboy who's about to compete?"

"I don't know, but I sure as hell don't want you telling me to break a leg."

She laughed at his disgruntled expression, then leaned farther over the fence. "Come here, then," she invited softly, "and I'll give you a kiss for good luck."

He glanced behind him to see if anyone was looking, then reined Danny Boy alongside the fence and leaned down. When he would have bussed her quickly, then withdrawn, Shelby caught his cheeks between her hands and held his face to hers, sweeping her tongue across his mouth, then slipping it between his lips. She heard his low groan, felt the shift from anger to desire as he cupped a hand at the back of her neck and took the kiss deeper.

"Our next steer wrestler is a cowboy from Texas, Troy Jacobs."

Hearing the rodeo announcer call his name over the loud speaker, Troy tore his mouth from Shelby's, his gray eyes questioning and dark with heat as he withdrew to meet her gaze.

"I'll be cheering for you," she promised.

"Yeah," he said, seemingly unable to tear his eyes from hers. "Thanks."

"Better hustle, buddy," Chico warned.

Troy glanced quickly at Chico, then back at Shelby, easing his hand from behind her neck. "Yeah, I guess I better." Gathering up the reins, he backed his horse a couple of steps, then grinned and tipped his hat to Shelby as he spun the horse around and spurred him toward the chute.

Shelby clasped her hands around the fence rail, her heart soaring wildly as she watched him ride away. But when she caught a glimpse of the steer penned inside the chute and the size of his horns, she dug her nails into the rail, her fear returning.

Shifting her gaze to Troy, she watched him back Danny Boy into the box and heard the *click* of the barrier being clipped into place. With her eyes locked on Troy's face, her heart in her throat, she watched him jerk his chin, signaling he was ready.

She jumped at the gunshot sound of the chute springing open, then held her breath as first the steer, then Yuma, then Troy streaked out into the arena, their entrances only split seconds apart.

"Oh, Lord, please, keep him safe," she prayed under her breath as she watched Troy lean out of the saddle and over the horned steer's back. Then he was on the ground, his hands and arms locked around the animal's horns, his boot heels kicking up clouds of dust as he dug them into the plowed dirt in an attempt to stop the steer. Danny Boy raced on across the arena, riderless, the saddle's empty stirrups flapping wildly at the horse's sides.

She closed her eyes, unable to watch, then snapped them open again when she heard a collective gasp rise from the stands. Troy lay on the ground with the steer half on and half off of him, his arms locked tightly around the steer's horns.

"What happened Chico?" she cried.

Chico made the sign of the cross. "He took a horn in the face."

Her breath froze in her lungs. "Oh, God, no. Please," she whispered. "Is he hurt?"

"Don't know yet."

Shelby watched, her heart in her throat, as Troy released his hold on the steer and rolled to his hands and knees, away from the animal. He dropped his head between his splayed arms. She saw the drips of blood that fell to moisten the plowed dirt, and terror like none she'd known in her life clawed its way through her. "Troy!" she screamed, and planted a sandal higher on the fence, intending to climb over.

But Chico caught her by the tail of her long skirt and tugged her back down, taking a firm hold on her arm. "They'll take care of him," he assured her.

"But he's hurt," she cried, trying to pull free. "I've got to help him."

"See," Chico said, pointing to the arena. "He's getting up. He'll be okay."

Shelby grabbed for the fence, pressing her face against the gap between the splintered rails, and watched Troy haul himself to his feet. He staggered two steps, and she choked back a sob just as Yuma appeared, ducking a shoulder beneath Troy's arm and leading him away.

Whirling, she raced toward the rear gate to meet them.

By the time she'd pushed her way through the crowd of people gathered there, Yuma had propped Troy up on a bale of hay. He sat with his head tipped back against the fence, his arms flung wide, his face as white as chalk. Blood poured down the right side of his face from a slash at the corner of his brow and soaked the front of his shirt.

Dropping to the ground at his feet, Shelby caught his hand in hers and squeezed.

He opened his eyes and looked down at her. "What was my time?"

"Your time?" she repeated dully.

"Yeah. I threw him. What was my time?"

"Four-point-two, buddy," Yuma interjected, squatting down to put his face level with Troy's. He glanced over at Shelby and shot her a wink. "But I think that steer will probably demand two of those seconds back, seeing as he got in a pretty good lick himself."

"Like hell," Troy grumbled, and touched a finger to his

eye. "Damn," he swore, wincing, when his fingers hit the torn flesh.

Shelby caught his hand in hers, pulling it from the wound, and rose to sit on the bale beside him, brushing his hair away from the cut. "Yes," she said, her voice trembling, "and I'm going to demand one of those seconds myself, since you broke your promise to me."

"What promise?" he asked, squinting at her to keep the blood from dripping into his eye.

"You promised me that you wouldn't get hurt," she reminded him, struggling to keep the tears at bay.

"I'm not hurt," he argued. "Just a little scratch. Where's my horse? Gotta haze for Yuma." He tried to stand, but sank weakly back to the bale of hay, groaning. "Just need a minute to catch my breath," he said, and swallowed hard.

"What you *need* is a doctor," Shelby told him firmly. She glanced up at Yuma.

"There's a medic right here and waiting," Yuma said before she could demand one. He stepped aside, and the medic moved into his place.

"Caught you a good one, huh, Troy?" the medic said as he leaned over him to examine the cut. "Came damn close to gouging out your eye."

Shelby felt her stomach roil, and wrapped an arm around her middle and a hand over her mouth, feeling the nausea rising.

"You gonna be sick?" Yuma asked.

"N-no," she whispered, afraid that she was. "I'm just—" She clamped her lips together as dots swam before her eyes. She swayed, heard a shout, felt herself falling…then everything went black.

"You're sure you're okay?"

Shelby swatted at the arm Troy tried to wrap around her, vying for control over who would help whom up the stairs.

"I'm fine," she told him irritably. "*You're* the one who was injured."

"You passed out."

She pursed her lips, ashamed of her weakness. "I did *not* pass out."

"You damn sure did. Would have fallen off the bale of hay, if I hadn't caught you."

"I didn't pass out. I…I simply lost consciousness for a moment."

"More like ten minutes. Scared the hell out of me."

"Well, you frightened me first."

They paused at the top of the motel's second-story landing and both took deep, shuddery breaths, turning to look at each other.

Feeling the tears coming again, Shelby tried to blink them back. "I don't think I've ever been more frightened in my life," she whispered, feeling the reaction setting in.

He wrapped his arms around her and drew her to his chest. "Me, neither," he murmured weakly.

"Not for myself," she cried, pushing from his embrace. "I was frightened for you!"

He stared at her in bewilderment. "Damn, Shelby. It's just a little cut."

"A little cut!" she all but screamed at him. "For heaven's sake, Troy, it took twelve stitches to close it. You came very near to losing your eye."

"But I didn't lose my eye," he reminded her, then dropped his arm around her shoulders again and turned her toward their room, his gait slow and a little unsteady. At the door he stopped and worked the key card from his pocket. He jabbed twice at the slot, before Shelby snatched it from his hand.

"Men," she muttered under her breath. "You've got more testosterone than brains."

Chuckling, Troy pushed open the door. "I'd say you

have a fair share. You were really giving that medic hell about not leaving any scars. Thought Yuma was going to have to pull you off of him there for a minute."

Shelby closed the door behind them and tossed her purse on the dresser, embarrassed by the reminder of her less-than-charitable behavior to the medic who'd cared for Troy. "I was concerned for your welfare," she replied with a lift of her chin.

"And I was concerned for yours," he reminded her pointedly.

"Don't start with me again," she warned. "I told you I'm fine." Lifting a hand, she stopped him before he could argue the point with her. "I refuse to discuss this any further. We need to get you into bed."

Scowling, Troy dropped down on the side of the bed, intending to rest just a minute before attempting to undress, but ended up falling to his back and flinging his arms wide. The pain pill the medic had offered and Shelby had insisted that he take was making him woozy.

"Lift up your foot," she ordered.

"I can take off my own damn boots," he grumbled.

"Yes, when you're not weak as a kitten, I'm sure you can. Now lift up your foot."

Deciding that arguing with her was pointless, he closed his eyes on a sigh of defeat and lifted his leg, then frowned when he felt something soft swish across his thigh. Raising his head, he opened one eye and found himself staring at the rounded curves of Shelby's back side, her full skirt bunched beneath her hips and cascading down both sides of his leg. She grunted and tugged, but the boot refused to budge. Wanting to help, Troy lifted his other foot, planted it against her rear end and gave it a shove, sending Shelby stumbling forward.

She whirled to glare at him, tossing the stubborn boot aside.

"I was just trying to help," he said, trying not to laugh.

Pursing her lips, she stomped back to the foot of the bed and grabbed his other leg, wrapping her hands around the heel of his boot. She tugged, grunting and groaning, and stumbled back a step when the boot gave way. Tossing it aside, she planted her hands on her hips. "Take off your clothes."

Enjoying this unprecedented display of temper and loving the fire that blazed in her blue eyes, he couldn't help teasing her a little. "No, please," he insisted, "ladies first."

She huffed a breath and dropped her hands from her hips, curling them into fists at her sides. "I've had about all I can take for one night. Now drop those jeans!"

Chuckling, Troy pushed himself to a sitting position, then sat there a moment, frowning as the room spun around him, unable to remember why he'd made the effort.

"The jeans," Shelby reminded him sharply.

"Oh, yeah." He rose, weaving precariously, unfastened his buckle and pushed down his zipper. Hooking his thumbs at the waist of his jeans, he gave them a shove, then dropped weakly down on the bed. Spent by the effort, he fell back on the mattress and threw his arms wide.

Standing at the foot of the bed, scarce inches from his sprawled legs, Shelby gulped, then swallowed, her gaze frozen on the jeans and briefs bunched around his ankles. She'd told him to take off his clothes, but she hadn't meant everything! Not his briefs, too!

Her mouth suddenly dry, she wet her lips and slowly lifted her gaze, trailing it cautiously up the swell of calf, over the hump of his bent knees, and along his muscled thighs until it rested at the juncture of his thighs and the shadowed cave created by his shirttails. Not wanting to look, to even think about what lay hidden inside that cave, she took a hesitant step closer to the bed.

"Troy?"

When he didn't respond she sank to a knee and lifted his foot, gently pulling the jeans and briefs from around it, then did the same for the other foot. Drawing a deep, shuddering breath, she rose, tossing his clothes aside, and her gaze went unerringly to the shadowed cave. As she stared, unblinking, he groaned, then shifted, dragging one arm up to cover his eyes, the other to lay low on his abdomen. Her breath hitched, then burned in her lungs as she realized the movement had tugged up the tails of his shirt.

She closed her eyes and inhaled deeply, willing herself not to look...but opened them again, unable to resist the temptation. Dark, coarse hair swirled upwards from his thighs and thickened between his legs, shadowing the heavy male sac that lay beneath. From the dark nest, she trailed her gaze higher to the staff that jutted from the springy curls, swallowed hard, then traced its length to where it curled, limp, against his groin.

Transfixed by the sight of his sleeping sex, she inched closer, bracing a hand on the mattress as she climbed up to sit on the bed beside him. She'd never seen a man so fully exposed before...at least not with the freedom to study one as openly as she did now in the soft lamplight. Derrick had always turned off the lights before removing his clothes, and had donned pajama bottoms after they'd made love.

Love.

Even as the word formed in her mind, she shunned it, casting it aside, knowing that what she had experienced with Derrick had nothing to do with love and everything to do with sex. He had wanted her, wooed her until she'd slid willingly into his bed. But he'd never loved her. He'd never squeezed her hand when she needed reassuring or wiped her tears when she cried. He'd never fought for her or defended her or even worried about her. He'd never driven all night to fulfill an obligation he'd made to her or sacrificed his own name to protect hers. He hadn't cared one whit about her or the baby that they had made together....

But Troy had. He'd done all those things and more.

Dragging a hand beneath her eyes, she shifted her gaze higher, humbled by the strength portrayed in the breadth of his wide chest and the kindness and tenderness in the heart that lay beneath the hard pads of muscle.

Her hand trembling, she reached out to him. "Troy? Sweetheart. You need to get underneath the covers."

He grunted, then lifted his arm from his eyes and squinted at her. "What?"

She rose to her knees, pulling the spread back. "You need to get under the covers. You'll get a cramp sleeping with your legs hanging off the bed like that."

He grunted again, but shifted, bracing his hands beside his hips and heaving himself higher up on the bed, then with a sigh, dropped his head onto the pillow.

A tender smile trembling at her lips, Shelby spread the sheet over him and tucked it at his hips. As she did, she saw the dried blood staining his shirt and froze, reliving again the horror and the fear she'd experienced when she'd seen him kneeling in the arena, blood dripping from his face. Wanting to remove the reminder, she reached for the first button, worked it free, sniffed, then moved on to the next.

"Shelby?"

She glanced up to find Troy's eyes open and staring at her. "Yes?" she said, sniffing again.

"Why are you crying?"

She dragged her wrist beneath her eyes and reached for the next button. "I'm not."

"Yeah, you are." He closed his hand over hers, stilling their movements. "Don't cry, sweetheart. I'm okay."

"I know you're okay," she said tearfully, then gulped a breath, sweeping her fingers beneath her eyes. "But you could have been seriously injured."

"But I wasn't," he reminded her gently. When his assurance brought on more tears, he lifted the sheet and opened his arms. "Come here."

Her breath hitching, she crawled beneath the covers and curled against his side, burying her face against his chest as he tucked the sheet around them both.

"You don't need to worry about me," he soothed as he stroked his hand down her hair. "I've survived a lot worse than this."

"Not since I've known you," she replied, tightening her arm around his waist, as if to protect him from further harm.

"Yeah, well, how 'bout if I promise to never get hurt again?"

She sniffed, dragging a cheek against his chest to wipe her tears. "I'm going to hold you to that promise."

He chuckled, still stroking her hair. "Deal. Now, close your eyes," he murmured sleepily. "You need your rest."

Shelby lay still beside him, knowing that he needed rest more than she but finding comfort in the feel of his fingers combing through her hair. His fingers slowed after a moment, then stopped altogether, his palm coming to rest heavily at the base of her neck.

Careful not to disturb him, she tilted up her face to peer at him. The strong, square jaw, shadowed with a day's growth of beard. Lips full and relaxed in sleep. Thick, dark lashes that curled against his cheek. The strip of bandage that concealed the line of stitches at the base of his right brow.

She touched a finger to his cheek just below the bandage, and her heart tightened in her chest.

When had he grown to mean so much to her? she wondered, feeling the tears gathering in her throat again. And what would she do with these feelings when their week together came to an end?

Seven

"Troy?"

He grunted, then shifted closer to the body curled against his side, not wanting to wake up for fear he'd lose this warm feeling of contentment. "Hmm?"

"Troy. The baby just moved."

He flipped open his eyes to stare at the dark ceiling, then slowly turned to look at Shelby. With her head resting in the curve of his shoulder, her face only inches from his, he could see the wonder in her blue eyes, the awe.

"Moved?"

"Yes," she whispered and rolled to her back. Taking his hand, she pressed it against her stomach. "Feel it?"

He lay there, frozen, his hand curved beneath hers over the slight swell of her stomach, unable to breathe. Though he tried hard to concentrate, he could think of nothing beyond the heat seeping into his palm, the softness of the flesh beneath the dress's thin fabric, the intimacy of his hand's position.

"Did you feel it?" she whispered.

"N-no," he said uneasily. "I didn't feel anything."

Frustrated, she shifted, adjusting his wide hand lower on her abdomen. He sucked in a breath through his teeth when his hand bumped against her pelvic bone and the length of his little finger brushed the cushy rise of her femininity.

"Did you feel it that time?"

Oh, he felt something all right, he thought, gulping, as he stared at her shadowed profile. But he was sure it wasn't what she had intended. Suddenly dry-mouthed, he nervously wet his lips, wondering if she had any idea the torture she was putting him through. Lying beside her in the darkness, nearly drunk from breathing her womanly scent, his hand lying intimately beneath hers with the rapid beat of her pulse thrumming seductively against his palm, he could think of nothing more satisfying than rolling over and claiming more than just a touch.

He shook off the lusty thought, sure that she didn't have a clue the effect she had on him and, worse, would be horrified if she did. He shifted his gaze to their joined hands, watching them rise and fall on her abdomen with each excited breath she drew.

He felt something stir beneath his palm, a featherlight flash of movement so slight he would have missed it or, at the least, disregarded it, if he hadn't heard Shelby's sharp inhalation of breath at the exact same moment.

"There!" she cried, pressing his hand more firmly against the spot as she turned her face to his. "Did you feel it that time?"

He swallowed hard at the excitement he saw in her eyes, the absolute radiance of her smile. "Yeah," he said slowly. "I felt it. Is that normal?"

"Yes. I've felt it before, but never so strongly."

She turned her face to the ceiling again, and he thought

he saw tears shimmering in her eyes as she closed both of her hands over his and hugged it to her stomach.

"Sometimes it doesn't seem real," she whispered almost guiltily, "like a dream that I'll wake from. Then I feel him move and I know that there really is a baby there. A miracle," she said, turning to peer at Troy in the darkness. "Two seeds coming together to create a human life. It's so hard to believe, yet it's happening right inside of me."

Though he had never given it much thought before, with his hand held tightly over the swell of her stomach, his palm still tingling from a brush of contact with that miracle, that new life, Troy thought he understood what she meant, how she must feel. Oddly, he felt much the same way. The baby had never been real to him. It was simply a "thing," the reason behind Shelby's need for a husband, the tie that bound their lives together, if only temporarily.

But he felt something else, too. Something he was sure that Shelby didn't feel.

A resentment that it wasn't his seed that had joined with hers to create that miracle.

Shelby's smile slowly melted as Troy's face turned to stone. "Troy? What is it? What's wrong?"

He jerked his hand from beneath hers and turned away. "Nothing's wrong."

She rolled to her knees, kneeling beside him and looking down at him. "Yes, there is," she insisted. "You're angry. Was it something I said? Something I did? I only wanted you to feel the baby."

He glared at the ceiling, refusing to look at her or reply.

She laid a hand on his chest. "Troy, please," she pleaded, then jumped, sucking in a startled breath, when his hand lashed out, his fingers closing like steel around her wrist.

"Don't," he grated out.

"D-don't, what?" she asked in confusion.

He shoved her hand from his chest and rolled to his side, turning his back to her. "I'm not a monk, dammit, who's taken a vow of celibacy. I'm a *man*. And a man can take only so much."

Shelby stared at the wall of his back, too stunned to speak. She'd aroused him, she realized slowly, then opened her hand to stare at it, unable to believe that she'd done so with such an innocent gesture. Yet, she'd angered him, too. But how? Why? All she'd wanted to do was share with him her excitement at feeling the baby's movement.

Sinking her teeth into her lower lip, she curled the hand into a fist, realizing that he must have found her touch repulsive. "I'm sorry," she murmured. "I didn't mean to...to tease you. I only wanted to share my excitement with you."

She heard as well as felt the vibration of the frustrated groan that welled from deep inside him as he rolled to his back. He dragged a hand down his face, then dropped his arm wearily to his side and turned to look at her.

"I wasn't accusing you of teasing me. It's just that—" He clamped his lips together, then swore. "Dammit, Shelby, don't cry."

She ducked her chin, blinking rapidly. "I'm not crying."

He pushed himself up to an elbow. "I'm not mad at *you*," he said, trying his damnedest to keep the frustration from his voice. "It's the situation I'm mad at."

When the tears continued to fall, Troy felt a rage swell within him, a rage that had nothing to do with her tears, but had everything to do with her and the damnable situation they were trapped in. "Do you have any idea how much I want to touch you?" he said, his voice rising to match the level of his frustration. "To have you touch me? How hard it is for me to lie here beside you and want you so bad it hurts, and know that I have no right to even think such thoughts about a lady as fine as yourself?"

Seeing her eyes widen in shock, he groaned and dropped back down on the bed and draped an arm over his eyes, wishing he hadn't exposed so much of his feelings to her, convinced that he'd now given her every reason she needed to be frightened of him. "Go back to sleep, Shelby. Forget what I said."

After a moment he felt the mattress shift and thought that she was doing as he'd suggested, prayed that she was...but froze when he felt the tremble of her fingers on his chest again.

"I didn't think you felt anything for me but a sense of responsibility."

Slowly he lifted his arm to look at her. "Why would you think a thing like that?"

She dropped her chin in shame. "Because I'm—because I'm—"

"Because you're pregnant?"

She lifted her gaze to his, her eyes filled with tears. "Y-yes. I didn't think you'd want a woman who was... soiled."

The term sounded so much like something her puritanical preacher-daddy would say that Troy was sure that was where she'd gotten the notion. And he wouldn't have her thinking such a thing about herself.

He pushed himself to an elbow again and placed a knuckle beneath her chin, forcing her gaze to his, determined to set her straight. "You're not soiled, Shelby," he told her firmly, "and don't let anyone ever try to convince you otherwise. There were other choices you could have made when you found out you were pregnant, but you chose the tough one. You chose to keep your child."

He dropped his gaze to her stomach, thinking about the flutter of movement he'd felt there, the sign of life he'd witnessed firsthand. A miracle she'd called it, in spite of all the emotional strain, the trauma, placed on her by choosing to keep the baby.

Sighing, he reached out and splayed a hand over the slight swell, molding its shape, thinking of the man who had planted the seed there, the one who had left her to deal with the results all alone. "I just wish it was my seed that had joined with yours," he murmured, "and that it was my baby that was growing inside you."

She pressed her fingers against her lips, tears filling her eyes again. "Oh, Troy."

He glanced up at her, unaware that he'd voiced the admission out loud, yet he knew it was true. He did wish it was his baby she carried. And he wished that their marriage wasn't a temporary one. But he knew that was impossible. Worse, he knew. Shelby deserved better than a man like him.

But before he could tell her that, she was wrapping her arms around his neck and pressing her wet cheek against his.

Sure that his heart would break if she shed one more tear, he rolled to his back, bringing her with him. With an arm braced around her, holding her against him, he tucked her head beneath his chin and stroked a hand down her hair. "It's gonna be okay, Shelby," he whispered, his voice husky. "I'm gonna make damn sure everything's okay for both you and your baby."

He held her for what seemed like hours, murmuring words of comfort, stroking her silky hair, soothing her as best he knew how.

"Troy?"

"Yeah?"

"You said it was hard for you not to touch me, yet you're touching me now."

"Yeah, I am," he said wryly. "But this isn't the kind of touching that I was talking about."

She slipped a hand between them, resting it over his heart. "It's been difficult for me, too," she admitted softly.

He tucked his chin back to peer at her, and Shelby saw the surprise in the gray depths. Holding his gaze, she smoothed her hand across his chest, traveling a slow journey from nipple to nipple. A shiver chased down her spine as the dark hair that swirled around each tight knot chafed against her palm, as the thundering beat of his heart quickened that of her own.

"You have a beautiful body," she whispered. "So muscular, so powerful. You have no idea how badly I've wanted to touch you in this way."

"Shelby."

There was a warning in her name as he spoke it, as well as a plea. She looked up at him, knowing that she would heed neither. She wanted him as badly as he professed to want her. "There's no sin in a woman wanting her husband, is there? Or in a man wanting his wife?"

"Shelby."

Her name came out on a groan this time as he rolled to his side and leaned over, claiming her mouth with his. He shifted, forcing her to her back and bringing his body alongside hers. "If there's a sin in it," he murmured against her lips, "then I would already be burning in hell." He nipped at her lower lip, then soothed the spot with his tongue. "And I'd welcome the punishment, because I've wanted you since that first night in your apartment when I slept beside you."

His confession surprised Shelby and was all the assurance she needed. She smoothed her hands down his sides, feeling each rib, each ripple of muscle, the strength. "Make love with me, Troy," she whispered.

He froze, not trusting his ears, then drew back far enough to look at her. "Are you sure?"

She lifted her hands and drew his face back to hers. "Yes. Never more sure of anything in my life."

"I don't want to hurt you," he murmured against her lips. "I'd die before I hurt you."

"You won't. You couldn't."

He dropped his forehead against hers, knowing he had no right to take advantage of the gift she offered him, but knowing, too, that there was no way he could refuse her. Not when he wanted the same damn thing. "You're sure about this?" he asked, lifting his head and searching her eyes for any doubts, knowing that her uncertainty was all that could stop him.

Smiling tremulously, she nodded her head. "Positive."

He sat up and drew her to a sitting position, as well, and reached for the first button of her wrinkled dress. As he did, he saw the bloodstains and knew they were from his own wound. "I ruined your dress."

She joined her hands with his, as anxious as he to be rid of the restrictive garment. "It doesn't matter."

"I'll buy you another one. Ten," he insisted, pausing long enough to seal the promise with a kiss.

With the buttons at last freed, he slipped the dress from beneath her hips and over her shoulders, while she dealt with her bra. Then he tossed both to the floor. "Damn," he murmured and sank slowly back on his heels, staring. "You're prettier than I'd even imagined."

Blushing, she crawled the short distance that separated them and wrapped her arms around his neck. Drawing him down to the bed with her, she used his body to shield her own from his probing gaze. "That cut near your eye must have affected your vision," she scolded, "because there is nothing pretty about a pregnant woman's body."

He braced himself above her with one arm, afraid to put his full weight on her. "There's nothing wrong with my vision. It's twenty-twenty."

"It's the drugs, then," she insisted, avoiding his gaze by brushing his hair away from the bandage that covered his stitches. "They must not have worn off yet, because I know I'm not pretty. I'm fat."

The fact that she couldn't look him in the eye told him a lot about her experience—or lack there of—with men, and hinted strongly at her shyness about her own nudity, which he found surprising, considering her current condition. It also made him wonder about the man who had taken her virginity and what kind of lover he'd been, what kind of care he'd taken with her.

"My head is clear as a bell," he said, and splayed a hand across her belly, hoping to prove to her that he found her body anything but repulsive. His touch brought her gaze to his, and he saw the insecurities there, as well as the heat.

Knowing he needed to resolve the first before he could even think about responding to the latter, he lowered his face over hers. "You're not fat," he assured her, nipping at her lower lip. "You're pregnant."

Shifting, he leaned to press his lips to the spot on her belly his hand had warmed and heard her sharp intake of breath. He glanced over at her and smiled. "And sweet. So sweet."

Her lips trembling, she reached out and laid her palm against the side of his face, stroking a thumb beneath his eye. "You are undoubtedly the kindest and gentlest man I've ever known."

He snorted a laugh. "Then you obviously haven't known very many." Before she could argue further, he dropped another quick kiss on her belly, then started working his way back up her stomach, alternately nipping at her bare skin, then soothing it with his lips. When he reached her breasts, he swirled his tongue around one nipple and bit back a groan when she shivered in reaction. Though he hadn't intended to stop there, he couldn't resist closing his mouth over the knotted flesh and drawing her in. He suckled gently, savoring her sweetness, her fullness, then, when she arched against him moaning her pleasure, he succumbed to his greed and drew her more deeply in.

Feeling his own need swelling, he lowered himself over her, laying flesh against flesh, heat against heat, and settled himself into the nest created by the juncture of her thighs.

"I'm not too heavy?" he asked, pressing kisses against the smooth column of her neck.

"No," she murmured breathlessly.

Taking himself in hand, he guided the tip of his staff to her opening and groaned at the moist heat he found there. He set his jaw, struggling for a control he feared he was close to losing. "I've been wanting you so much, I'm not sure how long I'll last," he said, feeling the need to both warn her and apologize for the brevity.

"It's okay," she whispered as she slid her hands down his back. She cupped his buttocks and drew him closer to her. "I'm ready."

In spite of her assurance, he dropped his forehead against hers, afraid to make that first move. "If I hurt you—"

"You won't."

"But if I do—"

"Troy, please," she said, her frustration obvious. Taking the choice from him, she arched beneath him, accepting him, taking him in.

Troy squeezed his eyes shut on a low moan as he slid inside her, savoring the feel of her velvety tightness sheathed around him. He was sure he'd landed himself in heaven. Nothing, he knew, could be sweeter or more pleasurable than this. Than her.

But when he felt the tension slowly leave her body and felt her soft sigh whisper at his ear, he flipped his eyes wide, then narrowed them in suspicion.

"Shelby?"

Her hands stroked lazily down his back and up again. "Yes?"

"You don't think that was it, do you, sweetheart?"

Her hands stopped midway down his spine. "It?" she repeated hesitantly.

"Yeah, you know, the end."

"W-well, yes," she stammered. "Wasn't it?"

Troy buried his face in the curve of her neck, unable to stop the chuckle that rumbled up from deep inside him. "No. Or at least it wasn't for me," he added, just in case he'd been wrong in assuming that she hadn't reached a climax, either.

"Oh-h-h."

The soft surprise in her voice made him laugh even harder, which worried him a bit, seeing as how he stood a chance of laughing his way right out of an erection.

"I'm sorry," she murmured in embarrassment. "I didn't realize…" When he continued to laugh, she huffed a breath and brought a fist down hard in the middle of his back. "Would you please stop laughing and tell me what I'm supposed to do!"

"Do?" he repeated, tucking his head in the crook of his arm to wipe the tears from his eyes. "You aren't supposed to *do* anything. You're just supposed to enjoy."

"Well, I was enjoying," she replied indignantly, "until your giggle box turned over."

Bracing his hands on either side of her face, he lifted himself up to look down at her. Seeing the hurt in her eyes before she turned her face away, he instantly sobered. He caught her chin and forced her gaze back to his. "I'm sorry, sweetheart," he murmured, and dropped a kiss on her lips. "I didn't mean to laugh. It's just that—"

"Just that what?" she snapped, still sounding miffed.

"Just that obviously you've never known the full pleasure a man can give a woman."

"The full—?"

He shifted, pushing himself deeper inside her, and her eyes went round.

"Oh-h-h," she murmured knowingly, then gasped a louder and stronger "Oh!" when he slipped a hand between them and stroked a finger along her feminine lips to her sensitive peak, making her legs convulse in reaction and heat shoot through her belly.

"Enjoy," he invited softly, smiling as he lowered his face to hers. He closed his mouth over hers and slipped his tongue between her parted lips and began to move both his hips and tongue in rhythm, setting the pace as he gently guided her in a slow, erotic dance. She quickly found the cadence and followed, matching him stroke for stroke, arching higher and harder against him with each new thrust.

Surprised by her passionate response, Troy struggled for control, perspiration beading on his chest and slickening her skin with each brush of his body against hers. He wanted to share the moment of gratification with her, yet he wondered if he could hold off that long. He'd never experienced such intense pleasure with a woman, such a burning need to satisfy one before himself, and he was determined to let her enjoy every sensation, every delight that a man could gift a woman with.

He watched the passion build on her face, felt her feminine walls tensing around him, the almost desperate arch of her hips against his, and knew that she was close to experiencing the ultimate high. With a low growl, he thrust hard and buried himself inside her. He held himself against her as she exploded, her walls clamping around his sex. Heard her cry out his name on a strangled sob that carried notes of both surprise and joy.

"Shelby," he gasped, the muscles in his arms burning as he strained to hold himself above her. "Look at me."

He watched her force her eyes open and slowly bring him into focus, her chest heaving beneath his.

"That was for you," he said, "but this one is for us."
He rose to his knees and thrust one last time, deeply, straining, watching her eyes widen, her lips part in surprise.
When he felt her walls begin to spasm a second time, he
caught her hands in his and wove his fingers through hers
as he slowly dragged them above her head, covering her
body with his. Closing his mouth over hers, he pumped his
seed into her, his own pleasure merging with hers. He shud-
dered, once, twice, feeling the sting of her nails cutting into
his hands. But the pain was anesthetized by the sweetness
of the sigh that warmed his ear as she melted beneath him,
muscle by slow muscle.

He started to move, fearing he would crush her with his
weight, but she tugged her hands from his and wrapped
them around his neck, holding him against her.

"No," she begged weakly. "Please don't go."

"But I'll crush you."

"No. Please. I want to be close to you."

Because he both understood and shared that need, he
rolled, taking her with him, and matched her body to the
length of his. With a sigh of contentment, she nestled her
head in the crook of his neck and a hand at his cheek.

"Troy?"

"Hmm?"

"That was the best 'the end' I've ever experienced," she
said shyly. "The very best."

Smiling, he tightened his arms around her. "For me, too,
sweetheart. For me, too."

"Oh, Troy," Shelby murmured as she climbed from his
truck, her eyes round and staring. "It's beautiful."

He stood at the hood of the truck, nervously watching
her face and measuring her reaction, hoping beyond hope
that she wasn't saying that just to make him feel better. He
wasn't sure why it was so important that Shelby approve

of his home, but he found his shoulders sagging with relief when she stopped beside him and shifted her gaze to his and he saw the sincerity in the blue depths, the true appreciation. He wondered why he'd ever doubted her.

"You like it?"

"Like it? I love it! You didn't mention that it was Victorian," she said, turning to gaze at the two-story house again.

He slung an arm around her shoulders and guided her up the bricked walk. "Victorian? Shoot, Shelby, it's just an old farmhouse."

"Oh, no," she cried, stopping him, too, as she turned to look at him in dismay. "Just look at all that gingerbread trim," she said, gesturing to the porch and the line of the roof, "the decorative molding. How old is it?" she asked, spinning to look at him again.

He lifted a shoulder. "I don't know. My grandparents lived here all their married life and my grandmother's parents before them."

"All that history," she said, turning to stare. "Just imagine the stories these walls could tell, if only they could talk."

Grateful that they couldn't, Troy urged her on up the steps. "Now you'd better prepare yourself," he warned. "The place has been closed up for a while." He stopped, then turned and marched back down the steps, pulling her along with him. "In fact, maybe we better check into a motel in town."

"Why, when we have this perfectly wonderful house to stay in?" she asked, jogging to keep up with his longer stride.

"You know," he grumbled, and gestured to her stomach. "You being pregnant and all. The smells might make you queasy."

She stopped, tugging him to a stop, as well, and laughed

as she wrapped her arms around his waist and hugged him to her. "The one thing I haven't suffered with this pregnancy is any nausea." She quickly stretched a hand to the picket fence post behind him and rapped her knuckles against it. "Knock on wood."

"Yeah, well, you make up for it with all the restroom breaks."

Laughing, she rose to her toes and pressed a kiss against the scowl he wore. "Sorry, but when you gotta go—"

"You gotta go," he finished dryly, then chuckled as he turned her around and aimed her for the front door again. "You're lucky Pete and Clayton weren't with us. If they were, and Clayton was behind the wheel, he would have driven off and left you at the last truck stop. He won't stop for anything short of filling up a gas tank."

Laughing softly, Shelby waited while he unlocked the door. "I'm going to have to meet these friends of yours. They sound like real characters."

"Oh, they are," he assured her as he pushed open the door. "Especially Pete. The man's about half-crazy. You never know what he'll pull next. Why I remember one time he—"

He stumbled back a step as Shelby turned and hurled herself against his chest. He wrapped his arms around her and locked his knees to keep them both from toppling over backward. "What the—"

But before he could finish the expletive, her mouth closed over his and stole his breath.

"What was that for?" he asked when he could breathe again.

She dropped her gaze, suddenly shy, to fuss with the button on his shirt pocket. "Just because."

"Because, what?"

She lifted her face and warmed him with a smile that

sent his blood racing. "Because I'm glad to be here with you."

She couldn't have said anything that would have pleased Troy more. Stooping, he caught her with one arm beneath the knees, the other at her waist, and swung her up into his arms.

"What are you doing?" she cried, laughing, as she clung to his neck.

He grinned down at her. "Carrying my wife across the threshold. Married twice, but damned if I ever thought to fulfill this particular tradition."

Eight

Later that night Troy stretched out on the quilt he'd spread on the ground and folded his arms beneath his head with a sigh of contentment. "I forget how pretty nights are here in Texas until I'm home again and witness one firsthand."

Lying beside him, Shelby turned to smile at him. "It is beautiful. So big," she said as she turned her face to the dark sky again. "Like the state, I guess."

"Yeah," he agreed, and rolled to his side. He curved an arm around her waist and snugged her hip up against his groin. "Everything is bigger in Texas," he added, grinning.

Laughing, she shoved at his chest. "Braggart."

He caught her hand and held it against his heart. "No brag, ma'am," he drawled. "Just fact."

She glanced over his shoulder, her laughter giving way to a wistful sigh as she stared at the sky. "There must be a million stars out tonight," she murmured, propping her cheek on her palm, awed by the sight. "I remember when

I was a little girl, I used to make a wish on them every night before I went to sleep.''

He lifted her hand from his chest and surprised her by pressing a kiss into the center of her palm. "And what did you wish for?''

She glanced at him as heat raced through her veins, then away, blushing. "Nothing."

"Yeah, you did," he insisted. "Tell me."

She smiled self-consciously, knowing he wouldn't rest until she'd shared her secret. "A prince."

His gray eyes danced with humor. "A prince for Princess Shelby," he teased. "And what did you plan to do with your prince, if your wish had been granted?''

"Live happily ever after."

Her reply came so quickly and was stated with such confidence that Troy could almost believe there was such a thing. Almost. "Do you really believe in that kind of stuff?''

"Yes," she said in surprise. "Don't you?''

He thought about that for a moment, then shook his head. "Maybe for some folks."

"Why not all? Happiness is an emotion, a state of mind. If a person wants to be happy, either as a couple or alone, then he or she *can* be happy."

If that were only true, he thought sadly. He'd never known that level of innocence, that purity of mind and spirit. Not even as a child. The brand given him at birth had robbed him of whatever innocence might have been his. He'd learned early the cold hard facts of life, the hardships, the injustices, the unfairness—had them literally beaten into him on a daily basis. He'd been forced to pay the price for others' mistakes, never knowing he had a choice in the matter. And though he'd tried his damnedest to protect those too weak to protect themselves, he'd paid a price for that, too, when he had failed.

She peered at him curiously. "You don't agree?"

He shook his head again and curled his hand around hers, making it into a fist within his larger one. "Nope."

She sat up, her forehead creasing in concern. "But you're happy, aren't you?"

As he looked up at her, the stars in the dark-blue sky formed a crown of sorts over her head…or, more likely, a halo for this angel. "I am right now."

"Why only now?"

"Because I'm with you."

She opened her mouth, then closed it again, melting, when she realized what he'd said. "Oh, Troy. That's really, really sweet."

"Sweet or not," he said with a shrug, "it's the truth."

She snuggled down beside him and laid a finger at the corner of his eye, just below the bandage. Smiling up at him, she dragged the finger lightly down his cheek. "You make me happy, too."

The shy admission tugged at his heart. Before he said something sappy, or something he would regret, he rolled to his side to face her, hooked a leg over hers and drew her closer to him. "Ever made love under the stars?"

Shelby's eyes widened, and a delicious shiver chased down her spine at the mere suggestion. "No. Are we going to?"

"Might."

She caught her lower lip between her teeth and lifted her head to glance uneasily over his shoulder. "But what if someone should see us?"

He laughed, the sound coming from deep in his chest. "Who's going to see? It's just you and me out here, a moon and about a zillion stars."

She glanced up at the diamond-studded sky, enchanted with the idea. "Okay," she said, returning her gaze to his.

He rolled to his feet and away from her, then held out his hand.

She took it, frowning, and allowed him to pull her to her feet. "What are you doing? I thought we were going to make love here under the stars?"

"We are." He reached for the top button of her blouse. "But first we need to get rid of some clothes."

She shivered as his knuckles brushed her bare skin, the reality of what she'd agreed to do slowly sinking in. She'd never walked naked in her own apartment, much less outside, where anyone might see her. Oddly, she found the idea thrilling, rather than frightening, and took a step closer, placing her hands on his chest. "This is so, so…"

"Risqué?" he suggested helpfully.

"Wa-a-a-y beyond risqué." She laughed, then slid her hands to his waist and tugged his shirttail from his jeans. "It's decadent."

"Decadent?" He frowned as he slipped her blouse over her shoulders, then peeled it slowly down her arms. "Mighty fancy word. What does it mean?"

"Sensual. Maybe a little carnal."

"Carnal?" He snorted and tossed the blouse aside, then dipped his head, searching for the closure on her bra. "That sounds an awful lot like a sin, and we've already resolved we're not sinning. We're married. Remember?"

Her fingers had been working while his were, and she spread his shirt open, splaying her palms against his bare skin, holding them there and absorbing his heat. Then, shifting her gaze to his, she swept her hands upward, pushing his shirt over his shoulders and stripping him to the waist. She stepped closer and pressed her bare breasts against his chest. "How could I forget?"

He groaned, and caught her low on her hips, tugging her against his erection. "You know," he said, his voice growing husky, "for a rank beginner, you sure learned how to bring a man to his knees mighty quick."

She laughed softly and slipped a hand between them, finding the tab of his zipper. "You're still standing," she reminded him.

He groaned as she drew the zipper down, her fingers grazing the length of his sex. "Yeah, but I'm growing weaker by the minute. Much more and you'll have me lying flat on the ground."

Feeling more brazen with each passing minute, she stepped closer, forcing him to take a step back. "Oh, but that's exactly where I want you."

Troy arched a brow, surprised by her newfound boldness. "Is that a fact?"

"Umm-hmm," she said, a devilish glint in her eye. "Now are you going willingly, or do I have to throw you?"

"Throw me?" He tossed back his head and laughed. "Though I'd like to see you try," he said, releasing the closure on her skirt, "I think I'll make this easy on you. On both of us."

He let the garment fall, to billow around her ankles, then dropped his jeans and briefs and kicked them aside. Taking her hand, he sank to his knees on the quilt and drew her down to kneel in front of him.

With his eyes on hers, he tucked his hands beneath her hair and lifted it, dropping it behind her shoulders and exposing her breasts to the night air. "Now that you've got me on my knees, what do you plan to do with me?" he asked, then dipped his head and closed his mouth over one breast.

"Do?" she repeated, her mind dulled by the rasp of his tongue on her tender flesh and the heat that flooded her body. "I-I'm not sure."

Chuckling, he used his tongue to lave the budded nipple, then circled wider.

She drew in a sharp breath and grabbed for his shoulders, clinging, as delicious shivers of sensation arced through her. "Do you have any idea how wonderful that feels?" she asked breathlessly.

"Tell me," he murmured, shifting to the other breast.

She closed her eyes, concentrating, wanting nothing to distract her from the pleasure. "Warm…moist…delicious. It makes me…ache."

"Where?"

"Everywhere. From here—" she touched a hand to her opposite breast, then dragged her fingertips slowly down her stomach "—to here," she said on a sigh, letting her fingers drift through the tight curls on her feminine mound. She opened her eyes to meet his gaze. "It's a wonderful ache, though. A raw, burning need."

"A need for what?"

"You." She surged closer, pressing her body against his. "I want you inside of me."

"Moving kinda fast, aren't you?" he teased, nipping playfully at her bottom lip.

"Not nearly fast enough." With a wicked gleam in her eye, she pressed her palms against his chest and gave him a push, forcing him to his back.

"Well, I'll be damned," he murmured, unfolding his legs and stretching them out on either side of her knees as he stared up at her in disbelief.

Kneeling now between his spread legs, she let her gaze move boldly over his body while she trailed her fingertips up the muscled lengths of his thighs. He jerked when she closed her slender fingers lightly around the base of his swollen staff.

"Careful there," he warned, then sucked in a breath through his teeth as she drew her fingers upward, tracing his length. "Mercy," he said, releasing his breath on a groan. "I don't know what's come over you, but I hope, whatever it is, it doesn't leave anytime soon."

"You like that?" she asked, her voice as silky as the stroke of her fingers as she slid her hand slowly up and down his length.

"Oh, yeah. I like, all right. I like that just fine."

"How does it feel?" she whispered, leaning over to touch her tongue to his tip. "Tell me."

He groaned and closed his eyes. "Good. Real good."

"Come on," she scolded gently. "You can do better than that."

He opened his eyes and lifted his head to frown at her. "You know I'm not any good with words."

"Yes, you are. Tell me."

Shaking his head, he reached for her, catching her under the arms. "Hell, I'm no good with words. But I will tell you this," he informed her as he drew her slowly up the length of his body, stopping when their sexes were aligned. "There is only one thing that I can think of that would feel better than having your hand wrapped around me."

"What?" she asked, nipping at his lips.

"This," he said, and pushed himself between the damp folds of her sex.

She closed her eyes, arching, purring her pleasure as he slid deeply inside. "Oh, yes," she agreed. "That does feel really nice."

He lifted his head and captured the back of her neck in a wide hand to guide her mouth to his. "Ride me, Shelby," he urged, teasing her tongue with his. "Take the reins and ride me as hard and fast you want."

The image in the invitation had Shelby's blood racing through her veins, even as fear gripped her chest. She'd never been so bold with a man as she was being with Troy tonight, never so free. But did she possess the skill to please him, as he'd pleased her the night before? Wanting desperately to give back to him, if only a modicum of the pleasure he'd given her, she pressed her hands against his chest and pushed herself up to sit high on his thighs, then groaned as the shift in position inadvertently took him deeper.

Searching for the courage, the boldness to lead, she began to move her hips against his. Slowly at first. Then faster with each grunt and groan she lured from him. With her gaze riveted on his face, measuring his response, she rocked up on her knees and lifted her hips, slowly drawing his length from her until only the very tip of his sex remained. She hung there a moment, suspended, thrilling at the sensations that pulsed through her, the heat that glazed his eyes. Then quickly she dropped, burying him deep inside her again. His groan of pleasure gave her the encouragement, the impetus she needed, and she began to move again, faster and faster, riding him with a wildness, an abandon that she'd never known, never suspected lay sleeping within her.

She arched her back and closed her eyes, tipping her face up to the night sky, offering herself as a sacrifice to the moon and stars, thrilling to the sensations that rolled in wave after wave through her body. She felt Troy's hands close around the fullness of her breasts, then slide to the peaks, the pinch of finger and thumb on her nipple sending electrical shocks spearing to her center.

Sure that she would drown in want, sucked under by the waves of sensations that continued to crash over her, threatening to steal her breath, she dragged her hands down his chest, her nails leaving a trail in their wake. "Troy," she begged. "Please!"

His eyes burned into hers as he rose, holding her hips against his. "Please, what?" he whispered. "Tell me what you want."

"You!" she cried. "Now. Please."

With a savage growl, he rolled, tucking her beneath him and claimed her mouth with his, spearing his tongue deep and swallowing her desperate pleas. Before she had time to adjust, he rolled again, dug his hands into her hips and thrust upward, burying himself deeply inside her.

Her breath caught, trapped in her lungs, as pleasure swelled inside her, rose to a sharp peak, then crested, shattering her senses and drawing her under. At the same moment, she felt his body tremble, heard his low growl. She clamped her legs tightly around him and dropped her head back, glorying in the heat and pulsing fullness that filled her, the moist heat of his seed as he spilled inside her.

Replete, sated, happier than she'd ever been in her life, she dragged her hands up her body, filled her hands with her hair, then pushed them higher, letting her hair tumble back to her shoulders and her fingers stretch toward the star-studded sky.

Then, laughing, she collapsed against his chest, covering her mouth with his. "Decadent," she murmured against his lips. "Definitely decadent."

Shelby hummed as she stretched across Troy's bed, tugging the sheet to the carved iron headboard, then carefully smoothing the wrinkles from it. Her step light, she waltzed to the foot of the bed, caught up the edge of the crocheted spread folded there and dragged it up and over the sheets, then fluffed the pillows and dropped them into place.

Pleased with herself and the world, she headed for the kitchen, hoping she had time to prepare breakfast before Troy returned from checking on his cattle. Though she had awakened when he had and offered to go with him, he'd insisted that she remain in bed and rest.

He was so protective of both her and the baby that she wanted to hug herself at her good fortune and scream in frustration at the same time. Shaking her head at the con-

flicting emotions, she passed through the living room, but
stopped when she saw the family Bible sitting on the coffee
table. The book was similar to the one her mother kept
beside her bed—tooled leather, aged to a soft patina
through frequent handling, its spine straining at the assort-
ment of items stuffed between its curled pages.

Curious to discover if the book offered as much family
history as her own family's Bible, she detoured to the sofa,
sat down and pulled the large, bulky volume onto her lap.

Smoothing her palm over the aged leather, she flipped
open the cover and found a crumbling rose pressed between
waxed paper. Scrawled on a scrap of paper beneath the
flower were the words, "Mother's Day, 1961." Knowing
by the date that the gift couldn't have been from Troy,
Shelby turned another page, and another, finding newspaper
clippings, printed programs from funerals, a rainbow of ribbons for achievements of unknown origin. The names
meant nothing to her, but she knew the items placed there
were cherished memories, probably of Troy's grandmother.

Turning another page, she picked up a document tucked
between the bible's yellowed pages. *Death Certificate. Tyler, Texas. Smith County. Sally Jean Jacobs.* Knowing the
person must be a relative of Troy's, she frowned, scanning
until she reached *Cause of death: drug overdose.* As she
silently read the words, gooseflesh popped up on her arms,
and she shivered.

A phone rang, startling her, and she quickly tucked the
document back into the Bible, replaced it on the table, then
ran for the kitchen. Seeing Troy's cell phone on the table,
she hesitated for a moment, wondering if he would appreciate her answering his phone. Catching her lower lip between her teeth, she picked it up.

"Hello?"

"May I speak with Troy Jacobs, please?"

Shelby winced at the feminine voice, wondering if she'd

made a mistake in answering his phone. "I'm sorry, but he isn't here right now. Could I take a message?"

"Yes, please. This is Mrs. Phillips from the All-Care Nursing Home. Could you tell him that we need him to come to the home as soon as possible?"

Shelby pressed a hand over her heart, fearing that something had happened to Troy's grandmother. "Is there an emergency?" she asked.

"No, not exactly," the woman replied. "But we need him here as quickly as possible. Would you see that he receives the message?"

"Yes. Yes, of course. I'll tell him as soon as he returns."

She pressed the disconnect button and laid the phone back on the table, her hands trembling, praying it wasn't bad news, then hurried to the window, searching for a sign of Troy's truck. Seeing it parked by the barn, she ran to the back door, down the steps and across the lawn. By the time she reached the barn, she was out of breath. "Troy!" she called, not seeing him. "Troy!" she called more loudly. "Are you in here?"

She heard the thud of footsteps overhead, then his face appeared in the loft opening, his hands braced on either side. "Up here. What's wrong?"

She wrung her hands at her waist. "You had a phone call. A Mrs. Phillips from the nursing home. She said you need to come as quickly as you can."

He closed his eyes on a groan and dropped his head between his arms. "Oh, God, no," he murmured.

Finding the nurses' station empty, Troy hurried down the hall, towing Shelby along with him. He stopped before a closed door, took a deep breath, then turned to Shelby. "It might be best if you wait here. I doubt she'll know who I am. Seeing you might confuse her more."

Shelby nodded her head and gave his hand a squeeze.

"Don't worry about me," she assured him, and waved him on. "Take care of your grandmother."

He dropped a quick kiss on her lips, then slipped inside the room, closing the door behind him.

Weak with worry, Shelby pressed her back against the wall and closed her eyes, offering up a fervent prayer. She jumped, flipping her eyes wide, when the door jerked open and Troy burst from the room, his face flushed with fury, his jaw set in an angry slash.

Frightened by his dark expression, she grabbed his hand. "Troy, what's wrong? What's happened?"

"They've tied her to the bed. They've never done that before. And, by God, I won't have it." He jerked free of her grasp and shoved past her. "Wait here. I'll be back."

She sagged weakly against the wall, her heart breaking for him as she watched him stalk away, his shoulders rigid, his hands curled into fists at his sides.

"Somebody, help me! Please help me!"

Shelby jumped at the muffled cry, then turned to stare at the door, realizing that the sound was coming from the other side. She spun to call for Troy, but he'd already disappeared around the corner.

She hesitated, remembering Troy's instructions to wait in the hallway. But the pitiful pleas for help continued, rising in volume and intensity.

Unable to bear the sound a moment longer, Shelby slipped inside the door and closed it softly behind her. A woman lay in a bed shoved against the wall, propped on pillows, sobbing, her white hair sticking up in tufts from a pink scalp, her eyes wild. When she saw Shelby, she started thrashing about, straining against the straps that bound her chests and wrists.

"Help me," she cried. "Oh, please help me. You've got to find Troy. Please! You've got to find Troy!"

Shelby hurried to the side of the bed, hoping to calm the

woman. "Troy's here," she soothed, smoothing a hand over the woman's hair. "He just...left for a minute. He'll be right back."

"He'll kill him," the woman sobbed pitifully. "I know he'll kill him this time."

Shelby frowned in confusion. "Who will he kill?" she asked uncertainly.

"Troy!" the woman wailed. "Samuel will kill him this time for sure. You've got to find him. Please," she wailed, "you've got to find him before Samuel does."

A hand closed on Shelby's arm, and she snapped her head around just as Troy shoved her to the side, taking her place at the side of the bed.

"I told you to wait outside," he growled under his breath.

Shelby stumbled back a step, shocked by his angry tone. "I'm sorry," she murmured. "I heard her crying and wanted to help."

"Wait in the hall," he said as he leaned across the bed, bracing a hand against the pillow on the far side of the woman's head. "It's okay, Granny," he said, his voice gentle now.

"Burt, please," she pleaded desperately, her fingers clawing at the sheets. "You've got to find Troy before Samuel does. Check the woods behind the house. He hides there sometimes." The woman's face crumpled, tears streaming down her face. "He'll kill him this time. I just know he will, Burt. He'll kill my Troy."

Rendered speechless by the woman's terrified pleas, yet baffled by their meaning, Shelby backed toward the door. *Burt?* She'd called Troy Burt. Who was Burt? And who was Samuel, the man his grandmother was convinced would kill Troy if he found him?

Feeling the doorknob hit her spine, Shelby reached behind her and turned it, then slipped through the doorway and out into the hall. Her heart racing, her mind churning, she pressed her back against the wall.

What did it all mean?

Nine

The ride back to the farm was pure hell for Shelby. Troy drove like a madman, his jaw set, his wide hands strangling the steering wheel, his eyes narrowed on the road ahead.

But it was his silence that frightened her most of all. He hadn't spoken a word to her since he'd emerged from his grandmother's room. Questions screamed through her mind, demanding answers that only he could give. Yet he stubbornly refused to offer any answers, and she couldn't bring herself to voice the questions, fearing she would upset him more.

When he finally braked to a stop in front of the farmhouse, she turned to look at him, unable to bear the forced quiet a moment longer.

"She called you Burt."

Scowling, he rammed the gearshift into Park and fell back against the seat, bracing a hand against the center of the steering wheel as he turned his head away to stare out the side window.

She waited, her nerves burning, willing him to answer, fearing she'd go mad if he didn't.

"Burt's her brother," he finally said, though he kept his face turned to the window, refusing to look at her. "He's been dead for over fifteen years. Sometimes she confuses me with him."

"And Samuel?" she asked, straining to see his face.

"Her husband."

The bitterness in his oddly phrased response spoke volumes. *Her husband.* Not *my grandfather.*

"Is Samuel…still living?" she asked hesitantly.

The fingers on the hand he braced against the steering wheel curled into a tight fist. "No."

"I'm sorry," she said, regretting the question. "I didn't know. Your grandmother seemed genuinely upset, as if she truly feared for your safety. I thought perhaps your grandfather was a present threat to you."

"Her mind's gone. She's living in the past."

She watched the tendons on his neck cord, the angry throb of his pulse beneath his skin, and knew that though his grandmother's wild rambling might be drawn from the past, what she said was real, pulled from a memory fractured by fear.

She couldn't imagine living with that kind of hate in a home, fearing for your life. And it had all happened so long ago. Troy couldn't have been more than a boy. Yet, he'd carried the anger, the resentment, the nightmares with him into adulthood.

"Troy," she said, and reached for him, wanting to offer him her comfort.

"Don't," he snapped, jerking away from her touch. He twisted open the door and jumped to the ground, slamming the door behind him.

Stunned, Shelby stared, feeling the sting of rejection as she watched him stalk to the front of the truck and around it. But when he yanked open her door and thrust out his hand to help her down, she slapped it away.

"Why are you angry with me?" she cried as she climbed down from the truck. "Why won't you talk to me? Why won't you let me help you? Comfort you?"

"Leave it be, Shelby," he warned, and slammed the door. "Just leave it be," he said again, and turned to walk away.

A rage unlike any she'd ever known tore through Shelby. She grabbed his arm and spun him around to face her. "I *won't* leave it be!" she screamed at him. "I want to help you, but I can't if you won't talk to me or allow me to touch you. I love you, Troy, and I can't bear to see you hurt."

His eyes sharpened, his face tensed, and she froze, realizing what she'd said, what she'd revealed. She watched a flash of regret streak through the gray depths so quickly she wasn't certain she'd seen it all.

Then his eyes turned stone-cold, and a mask slipped over his face, guarding his expression, his emotions, from her.

"You want to know about my family?" he asked, his voice deceptively quiet after the explosive anger before. "Well, I'll tell you about my family," he said, and took a threatening step toward her. "I'm a bastard. Never met my old man. Never even knew his name. He got my mother pregnant, then skipped out, leaving her to deal with me alone."

Shelby placed a hand between them, trying to stop his forward movement. "Troy, please. You're frightening me."

"Am I?" he asked, then snorted and took another step, penning her between the truck and the wall of his chest. "You don't know what fear is until you've lived with it day after day, never knowing when the next beating was coming or if it would ever end when it did come."

He leaned into her, bracing his hands against the truck window, one wide palm on either side of her face. "I killed my mother, Shelby."

"No," she whispered, and clamped her hands over her ears, refusing to believe that he could do such a thing. Not Troy. Not her kind and gentle Troy.

He laughed at her reaction, the bitter sound ludicrous in the cheerful sunshine that beamed down on them from a clear blue sky.

"That's hard to believe, isn't it?" He shoved his face close to hers, forcing her head back against the glass and her gaze to his. "But I did kill her, as surely as if I'd put a gun to her head. She wanted to die, was willing to face hell itself to escape her father.

"He called her a slut, a whore, for getting pregnant with me, and he never let her forget the shame he claimed she brought on the family name. She finally snapped. Couldn't take it any more. Decided to kill herself and me, too. Took her daddy's car down by the creek, jammed a potato in the tailpipe, settled us both inside and left the engine running."

Troy squeezed his eyes shut, seeing it all again as clearly as if it had happened that morning. He pushed away from Shelby with a growl and spun, digging his fingers through his hair. "But I ruined her plan. I didn't die with her. I got sick and crawled out of the car."

Sobbing, Shelby stretched out a hand, reaching for him. "Troy, you didn't kill her. She killed herself."

He wheeled to face her, his body trembling, his eyes gleaming with unshed tears. "I did kill her. I closed the door behind me and left her in that car to die alone. I hid in the barn, scared that he would find me. And he did find me," he said, whirling away again to hide the tears that brimmed. "And he beat me. Blamed me for her death, for bringing more shame on the family. He shifted onto me all the bitterness, all the hate and resentment he'd once shoveled onto her, and he made me pay for her mistakes, and mine, until the day he died.''

His chest heaved on a sob, but he set his jaw against it and fisted his hands at his hips, inhaling deeply, refusing to give in to the grief. When he was calmer, when he knew he could face Shelby and not crumble beneath the compassion he knew he'd find in her eyes, he turned to look at her again. ''Is that the kind of man you want to love, Shelby?'' he demanded. ''Is that the kind of man you want for the father of your child?''

Trembling, knowing that whatever answer she gave would be the wrong one, she gave him her heart. ''I love you, Troy.''

He stared at her a moment, his eyes boring into hers, searching, as if he wanted to believe her, needed to believe her. Then he snorted and shoved past her. ''Then you're a fool,'' he muttered. He wrenched open the door of his truck and leaped inside. Gunning the engine, he jerked down the gearshift and drove away, leaving Shelby standing in the yard alone.

Shelby didn't wait to see if Troy would return. She called a taxi, packed her bag, then wrote him a note. She wouldn't stay. Couldn't. Because if he didn't come back, she knew it would kill her. She'd foolishly given her heart once to one man who didn't want it. She didn't think she'd survive having it shredded to pieces and tossed back in her face a second time.

Blinded by tears, she stood in the living room, trying to think where to leave the note, a place where Troy would find it. A horn honked outside, and she glanced out the window just as the taxi pulled up out front.

With a last frantic glance around, she dropped the note onto the Bible sitting on the coffee table, then started for the door. She stopped, her heart freezing in her chest, and glanced back at the Bible, remembering the death certificate she'd found inside it earlier that morning. Her fingers slipped from the suitcase's handle and she ran back across the room, dropping to her knees beside the coffee table. Dragging the heavy book toward her, she opened the cover, and began to flip through the pages, frantically searching for the document she'd discovered that morning.

When she found it, she slipped it from between the worn pages of the Bible and sank back on her heels. Taking a deep breath, she opened the document, her hands trembling uncontrollably as she scanned for the date. Finding it, she mentally did the math, subtracting Troy's age from the date of the woman's death recorded there. Her breath hitched, and she pressed a hand at her breasts as she scanned further to read again, knowing it was his mother's death recorded there. *Cause of death: drug overdose.*

Hearing the taxi driver's impatient honk, she quickly closed the Bible and rose, pushing it back into place on the coffee table. With a silent prayer that her assumption was correct, she laid the death certificate on top of the Bible, then dropped her note on top.

After collecting her suitcase again, she crossed to the front door and closed it carefully behind her, before hurrying down the steps and across the lawn to the waiting taxi.

"I'm sorry to keep you waiting," she murmured in apology as she slid onto the back seat, placing her suitcase on the floorboard at her feet.

"Where to?"

She closed the door and swallowed hard, forcing back the emotion that choked her. "The Tyler airport."

With a nod, the driver put the car in gear and made a wide turn. "What time's your flight?"

"I don't have a reservation."

"A gambler, huh?" the driver said, and laughed.

"Yes," Shelby murmured, blinking back tears as she remembered standing before the slot machine in Las Vegas pressed against Troy's side while coins spilled onto the floor around their feet. "I'm told that I'm lucky."

The driver lifted a shoulder. "Probably won't need to rely too much on luck to catch a flight this time of day, so long as you're not in a hurry to get wherever it is you're going," he added judiciously. "You a friend of the Jacobses?" he asked curiously, peering at her in the rearview mirror.

"Yes. Troy's," she clarified, wondering if Troy considered her as such.

"Know him on sight, but that's about it," the man said, making the turn onto the highway. "But I knew his grandmother. Nice lady. Used to take her on her errands when Troy was out on the road. 'Course that was before she moved to the nursing home." He shook his head sadly. "Damn shame," he muttered. "And such a nice lady, too. Good heart."

"Yes," Shelby said absently, remembering his grandmother's hysteria, her desperate pleas for someone to save Troy. Oh, how she must have suffered, she thought sadly, her heart going out to the woman. The emotional strain, the physical danger she'd exposed herself to by placing herself between her husband and her grandson, in order to protect Troy.

Leaning forward, she touched a hand to the driver's shoulder. "Would it be too much trouble for you to swing by the nursing home before taking me to the airport?"

"No trouble at all," the man replied. "If you've got the money, I've got the time."

Not sure what awaited her on the other side of the door, Shelby eased through the small opening and peeked inside the room. She was relieved to see that Troy's grandmother was sitting in a wheelchair in front of the window and no longer strapped to her bed. "Mrs. Jacobs? May I come in?"

The old woman turned her head to peer at Shelby, then motioned for her to enter as she spun her wheelchair around. "I'd welcome something new to look at it. 'Bout stared a hole in this window here."

"You have a good view," Shelby said, nodding toward the window. "It's a beautiful day outside."

"That it is," the woman agreed with a nod. "Makes me wish I was out in my garden with my hands buried in a freshly plowed row."

In spite of her nervousness, Shelby found herself smiling, finding the woman's simple speech much like Troy's.

"Are you coming in or not?" the woman grumped, startling Shelby. "You're hanging on to that door tighter than a new hinge."

Blushing, Shelby stepped farther into the room. "I'm coming in, though I can't stay long," she added with regret. "I have a taxi waiting."

"A taxi, huh? Wouldn't be George Flatt behind the wheel, would it?"

"Yes, I believe it is," Shelby said, thankful that the woman's mind seemed clear at the moment.

"Watch him. He'll make a block or two that's not required, just to put some more time on the meter."

Shelby bit back a laugh. "I'll consider myself warned."

A frown knit the woman's brow, and she leaned forward to peer more closely at Shelby. "Do I know you?"

Shelby shook her head, embarrassed that she hadn't thought to introduce herself. "No. I'm Shelby. A friend of Troy's," she added hesitantly as she offered her hand.

A pleased smile spread across the woman's face as she gripped Shelby's hand between her gnarled ones. "A friend of Troy's, huh? Have a seat," she said, gesturing. "It's good to know that he's not spending *all* his time with those two good-for-nuthin' boys he travels with.''

Shelby pulled a chair from against the wall and sat opposite Mrs. Jacobs. "Pete and Clayton?"

The woman cackled, slapping her thigh. "So you know 'em, too, huh?"

"No. But Troy speaks of them often."

"They're good boys," she said with a brisk nod of approval. "Though I do have to give their ears a twist now and again to remind them of their manners."

"I can't speak for the other two, but you've done a wonderful job raising Troy. He's a fine man."

Mrs. Jacobs pulled a handkerchief from the pocket of her robe to dab at the tears that spurted to her eyes. "Had nothing to do with me," she said, shaking her head. "Troy turned out good in spite of his raising."

Reminded of the terrors they both must have lived with, Shelby eased forward in her chair. "How old was Troy when his mother died, Mrs. Jacobs?"

The woman dropped her gaze to twist the handkerchief around a stiff finger. "Five in years, but an old man in experience." She sighed and unwound the handkerchief. Drawing her hands to rest on the arms of the wheelchair, she settled her gaze on Shelby's. "He was more a parent to Sally Jean than she was a parent to him. Looked out for her when she didn't have the strength or gumption to look out for herself." She shook her head sadly, her eyes filling with tears again. "I loved that girl with all my heart, but I knew her weaknesses. Loved her in spite of them. But Samuel…" She shook her head again. "Well, maybe he loved her too much. Expected too much. I don't know," she said wearily. "But he turned mean. Like a rabid dog, chewing on his leg, causing his own pain."

"I understand that Troy's mother committed suicide."

"Yes. Guess she got to where she couldn't stand going

on living any longer. Was looking for a way to escape it all.''

''How did she die?''

''Drug overdose. Took a bunch of pills, then plugged up the exhaust pipe on her daddy's car and climbed in, rolling up all the windows real tight. Insurance, I guess, in case the pills didn't work.''

''But it was the pills that killed her, wasn't it?'' Shelby asked, needing to know for sure.

''Lord, yes! She took enough to kill a horse, much less a woman of her size.''

''Was Troy with her?''

Mrs. Jacobs frowned, peering at Shelby as if she had a screw or two loose. ''Law, no. He'd be dead if he'd been in that car with her.''

''You're sure?''

'''Course I'm sure. Why do you ask?''

Shelby shook her head, not wanting to burden the woman with the truth, knowing that no purpose would be served by Mrs. Jacobs learning that Troy had been in the car with his mother. ''It's just that you mentioned that Troy was protective of his mother. I thought perhaps he might have been with her.''

''No, though I think her death haunts him some. Blames himself for what she done.''

Shelby glanced at her watch, realizing the time. ''I guess I better go. I'm sure George will be growing impatient.'' She rose and offered her hand. ''It was nice visiting with you, Mrs. Jacobs.''

''Come again anytime.''

Impulsively Shelby leaned down and hugged the woman.

Mrs. Jacobs laughed and hugged her back. ''You be sure and give one of those hugs to Troy,'' she ordered, wagging a finger in Shelby's face. ''He needs lots of hugging. Didn't get near enough when he was growing up.''

Choked by emotion, Shelby could only nod. With a last wave she turned and hurried for the door.

It was almost midnight when Troy returned home. He parked at the side of the house and dropped to the ground, his blood running cold when he saw that the windows were dark.

She wouldn't leave, he told himself as he headed for the back door. Not Shelby. Please, God, not Shelby, too. She loved him. She'd told him so. In spite of all the things he'd told her, she'd said she loved him.

His heart hammering a hole in his chest, he shoved open the back door. "Shelby?" he called, and stopped, his heart seeming to stop, too, as he listened for her response. Hearing nothing but the low hum of the refrigerator's motor, he ran for the hallway and down it, stopping in the doorway to his bedroom and bracing his hands against the jamb as he stared at the neatly made bed.

"No," he murmured, swaying. "No!" he cried, and dropped to his knees, burying his face in his hands.

Troy plowed through the next day like a freight train running at full throttle, knowing he had to stay busy or else go crazy. He stacked hay, filling the barn's hayloft with the square bales he would need for winter feeding, and set a new fence post, replacing one that had rotted at the ground. He tore down a shed that had stood long past its prime, then staked out the foundation for a new, larger one to replace it. By the time dark settled over the landscape, he was whipped-down tired, and all but crawled into the house and into a hot tub.

He soaked for more than an hour, adding hot water when his bath grew cold, too tired to think, but finally climbed out when his skin began to look like a prune's. Wishing he could sleep, but knowing he didn't stand a snowball's chance in hell of accomplishing that, he wrapped a towel around his waist and padded barefoot to the living room. In hopes of drowning out the thoughts of Shelby that pushed at the edges of his mind, he switched on the television and dropped down on the sofa, propping his bare feet on the coffee table.

With a sigh, he reared back, bracing his hands behind his head, but jumped, startled, when the phone rang.

Bolting to his feet, he ran to the kitchen and snatched his cell phone from the table where he'd left it, his heart racing, hoping beyond hope that it was Shelby. "Hello!"

"Troy? That you?"

He sank weakly down onto one of the kitchen chairs. "Granny?"

"Yeah, sweetie, it's your granny. Mrs. Phillips let me borrow the phone at the nurses' station and looked up your number for me. I can't remember things like I used to, you know."

He almost laughed at the understatement, but feared if he did he'd end up crying. "Yeah, I know," he said gently. "Are you okay? Nothing's wrong, is there?"

"No, I was just a missin' you, so thought I'd call."

He pinched his lips together and blinked hard up at the ceiling, willing the clot of emotion from his throat. "I miss you, too, Granny."

"Had me some company today."

"You did? Who?"

"Sweet little gal. Can't recall her name right now, though. But she said she was a friend of yours."

Troy rose, holding a hand over the stab of pain in his chest, unable to breathe. "Was she a blonde? Sort of fragile looking?"

"Sounds like the one, all right. Is she your girlfriend?"

"Yeah. No." He dragged a hand down his face and

stared up at the ceiling, holding the phone to his ear. "She's just a friend, Granny. A good friend."

"You ought to slap your brand on that one, Troy. She looks like a keeper."

In spite of the fact that his heart was cracking wide open, Troy found himself laughing. "Yeah, Granny, she is."

"You eatin' right?" she asked.

"Yes, ma'am," he lied. He hadn't eaten a damn thing all day. Couldn't.

"That's good. A growin' boy like you needs to keep up his strength."

"I hope to hell I'm through growing," he said, grinning. "Much more and my feet'll drag the ground when I'm sitting in the saddle."

She cackled at that, the familiar sound making his grin widen, then she sighed. "Guess I better get off the phone. Don't want to run up a big bill."

"You call anytime you want," Troy told her. "I'll take care of the bill."

"You're a good boy, Troy. A good boy."

"I love you, Granny," he murmured, feeling the tears stinging his eyes.

"I love you, too, sweetie. Good night."

"'Night, Granny. Take care."

Firming his lips, Troy broke the connection and set the phone back down on the table, staring at it for a long moment, tempted to punch in another number. Before he could give in to the temptation, he heaved himself away from the table. Tucking the towel more securely at his waist, he headed for the living room.

As he dropped back down onto the sofa, he noticed papers lying on top of the family Bible. Wondering where they'd come from, he leaned over and picked them up. He started to slip them inside the Bible, then frowned as he recognized Shelby's handwriting on the face of the envelope. Tossing aside the other document, he ripped open the envelope and leaned forward, bracing his elbows on his knees as he flipped open the small sheet of paper.

Troy:

It's difficult to find the words to express to you what is in my heart, so please bear with me.

I'm going home. Not because I don't love you. I'm going home because I *do* love you. And because I do, I find it impossible to remain here with you and watch you suffer, knowing that you won't allow me to offer you the same comfort and understanding that you would offer to me if our situations were reversed.

Though I understand the guilt you live with, I know in my heart that you aren't responsible for your mother's death. But I also know that as long as you feel you are responsible, you will never be free to accept the love that I want so desperately to give to you. You called me a fool, and I suppose my actions in the past might support your claim. But I'm not foolish enough to remain where I'm not wanted. I want the "happily ever after" we talked about, but that is impossible unless love is both given and taken freely.

Reaching the end of the page, Troy dragged a hand down his face as he flipped the note over to read the other side.

Our relationship will continue in the vein that it was originally established—a purely business one. As soon as the baby is born, I'll contact you, so that we can make arrangements for our divorce.

I hope that all of this doesn't sound as cold and unfeeling as I fear. Please know that I am, and always will be, eternally grateful for the sacrifices that you have made for both me and my baby. As I've told you before, you're a good man, Troy. The best.

She'd signed it simply "Shelby."

Troy fell back against the sofa with a groan, holding the letter against his chest.

How was he supposed to respond to this? What could he possibly say?

Nothing, dammit! He couldn't respond at all. He loved Shelby. More than he loved life itself. But he could never tell her that. She was right. The guilt he bore for his mother's death would always be there between them.

He heaved himself from the sofa to pace across the room.

Didn't she understand that he didn't deserve the comfort and understanding that she wanted so badly to give him? He *was* responsible for his mother's death, dammit! He'd left her in that car to die alone. Over the years he'd replayed the scene in his mind a thousand times, trying to find a way to escape the guilt. But there wasn't any. The fact was that if he'd left the door open when he'd crawled out, or maybe dragged her out with him, he knew his mother would be alive today.

No. Shelby was right. He would never be free of the guilt. He would take it to his grave with him.

Furious that his past was cheating him out of accepting the most precious gift he'd ever been offered in his whole sorry life, he balled the letter within his fist and threw it as hard as he could. It bounced off the wall and landed on the sofa, rolling to a stop within inches of the document that had lain beneath the letter on the Bible.

Staring at the folded paper, yellowed with age, Troy frowned as he stooped to pick it up, wondering if it, too, had been left by Shelby. He thumbed open the fold, and quickly scanned the page, sinking weakly to the sofa as he realized what he held.

Death Certificate. Tyler, Texas. Smith County. Sally Jean

Jacobs. He scanned quickly to read the cause of death. *Drug overdose.*

He rose slowly, the typed words swimming before his eyes. "No," he murmured, shaking his head. Not drug overdose. His mother had died of carbon monoxide poisoning. He had been there. In the car with her. He'd watched her stuff the potato in the tailpipe. Sat with her while the engine ran, filling the car's interior with the deadly poisonous gas.

Even as he recalled each detail of that afternoon, his stomach roiled, his head ached and he grew dizzy, tasting again the bitter bile. He could hear his grandfather screaming at him, feel the blow to his cheek that had sent him flying backward, the scrape on his butt and legs when he hit the ground hard and skidded.

But maybe…

Knowing it was hopeless, probably futile, he strode to the kitchen and dug the telephone directory from the drawer. He set his mouth in a grim line, refusing to hope, and flipped to the Blue Pages. Holding a finger beneath the listing for the county coroner, he picked up the phone.

After punching in the number, he put the phone to his ear and took a deep breath, quickly releasing it when a male voice answered.

"Jim? Troy Jacobs. I need you to verify some information for me."

Jerked from sleep by a stab of pain in her lower abdomen, Shelby sat straight up in bed, her eyes wide, fear gripping her chest. Another pain ripped through her middle, and she cried out, bending double and wrapping her arms around her waist. She sat with her forehead pressed against her knees, panting, waiting for the pain to recede. When it did, she slowly sat up again and inhaled deeply, holding a hand against her middle.

The baby, she thought, feeling the panic rising. Something was wrong with the baby.

She had to get help, she told herself, forcing back the panic. She had to get to the hospital. She couldn't lose her baby. She couldn't!

Oh, Troy, she cried silently, choking back a sob. I need you. Oh, God, I need you!

Easing her feet over the side of the bed, she slowly pushed herself to her feet. Trembling, she took a step, then another, then stopped, bending double again when a pain ripped like a hot knife through her back and middle. Bracing a hand against the sofa, she fought to breathe, then widened her eyes when she felt a gush of warmth between her legs.

She stared down in horror as blood ran down her legs and pooled on the floor around her feet. Knowing she had to get help and quickly, she staggered to the end table and the phone. Fighting back the tears, the panic, she punched in her parents' number and waited through two rings.

"Cannon residence. Reverend Cannon speaking."

All hope of holding back the tears was lost at the sound of her father's voice. "Daddy," she sobbed. "You've got to help me. I'm bleeding."

"Bleeding? Shelby! What's wrong?"

She pressed her hand over her mouth, fighting back the hysteria, the dizziness. "Please, D-Daddy, come quickly. I'm l-losing the baby."

"Baby!" he cried. "What baby?"

The phone slipped from Shelby's limp fingers and clattered to the floor. She followed, grabbing for the edge of the table to break her fall. "Hurry," she sobbed, her voice muffled by her arm. "Oh, God, please hurry."

Knowing he would make better time flying than driving, Troy hopped a plane in Tyler and flew into the Phoenix airport, rented a car and hauled butt for Dunning, arriving there a little after one in the morning. He drove straight to Shelby's apartment, loped up the stairs and pounded on her door.

"Shelby!" he yelled. "Open up! It's me, Troy!"

He listened, resting his fist against the door for at least two seconds, then pounded again. "Hey, Shelby! Open up!"

When there was still no response, he spun, checking the drive below, and frowned when he saw that her car was parked beneath the security light. Swinging back around, he lifted his fist again, but froze just short of hitting the door when he noticed a dark pool of liquid just below the toe of his boot.

He knelt, dipped his finger in it and brought to his nose, praying he was wrong about its identity. His nostrils flared as the sharp, coppery scent hit his senses and he sagged, bracing a hand against the door to keep from falling. "Oh, God, no," he murmured under his breath. Dragging in air, he rose, looked around, hoping for some sign, some indication of what had happened, where Shelby might be.

Cursing, he loped back down the stairs to the rental car and gunned the engine, squealing tires as he backed the car from behind the building, then left a trail of rubber on the alleyway as he careened for the street.

He stopped at the preacher's house, swore when he found no one home, then climbed into the rental again and drove wildly in search of the hospital.

He found it three blocks from the church he'd married Shelby in and whipped into a slot reserved for a doctor, jumped from the car and raced for the emergency entrance.

At the nurses' station he skidded to a stop, his chest heaving. "Shelby Jacobs—Cannon," he clarified, unsure which name she might have used. "Is she here?"

The nurse stared at him in dismay. "Well, yes. She was admitted several hours ago."

"What room?"

"Room 112, but visiting hours are over. You'll have to come back tomorrow."

"Like hell," he growled, and spun for the double doors leading to the lobby.

"Stop!" the nurse cried, leaping to her feet. "Or I'll call security!"

"Call 'em," he tossed over his shoulder as he pushed through the doors. He jogged across the lobby, looking left and right for a sign indicating room numbers. Finding the wing he wanted, he raced for the doorway, burst through it, then down the hall, sliding to a stop in front of room 112. He hesitated a moment, gulping a breath and stuck out a hand to shove the door open.

It swung wide before his hand touched the sterile, white paint, and a nurse stepped through, then jumped back, startled. Pursing her lips, she stepped into the hallway and closed the door firmly behind her. "I'm sorry, sir," she said, "visiting hours are over."

Troy jerked his chin toward the door. "Is Shelby in there?"

"Yes, but you can't see her."

"Are her parents with her?"

"No. You just missed them. They left not more than five minutes ago."

"What happened to her? How is she?"

The nurse pressed her lips together. "You'll have to speak with the doctor about her condition."

"Where is he?"

"Home in bed by now, I would think."

At the end of his patience, Troy took a step toward the nurse. "That's my wife in there, and I want to know what's wrong with her, why she's here. Now are you going to tell me, or am I going to have to insist that you call that doctor and wake him up?''

The nurse shrank away, obviously frightened by his threatening closeness. ''She experienced a threatened abortion.''

''Abortion!'' Troy cried.

''Keep your voice down,'' the nurse ordered in an angry whisper. ''We have patients trying to sleep who need their rest.''

Fighting for a calm that he'd lost the moment he'd seen the blood on Shelby's stoop, Troy dragged a hand down his face. ''Please tell me that she didn't have an abortion.''

The nurse's brows shot up. ''Well, of course she didn't. The condition is spontaneous, usually brought on by severe stress.''

Troy dropped his head into his hand, banding his forehead between his spread fingers and squeezing, knowing the stress Shelby had suffered was his fault. ''The baby?'' he whispered. ''Is it all right?''

''The doctor would be the one to answer that question. But the bleeding has stopped,'' she was quick to say, when Troy sagged against the wall, groaning. ''And the sonogram showed a strong fetal heartbeat.''

Troy dropped his hand and turned his head to stare at the door, tears blurring his vision. ''And Shelby? Is she going to be all right?''

''She's weak from loss of blood, and was rather upset, when her parents brought her in. But the doctor gave her a sedative and she's resting quietly now.''

''I have to see her,'' he said, then turned his desperate gaze on the nurse.

She opened her mouth as if to argue the point, then closed it with a snap. She turned away with a haughty lift of her chin. ''If someone enters a room when I'm not looking,'' she said primly as she marched down the hall toward her station, "then there's very little I can do about it, now, is there?"

Releasing his breath, Troy murmured his thanks, then pushed open the door and slipped inside. He let the door shush closed behind him as his gaze went to the bed. What little light there was in the small room came from a fixture over the sink, but it was enough for him to make out Shelby's shape. She looked so small lying there, so frail.

With his heart thumping against his ribs, his gaze frozen on her pale face, he crossed the room, keeping his tread light so as not to disturb her. When he reached the side of the bed, he took her hand in his and leaned over her to press his lips against her forehead. "I'm so sorry, Shelby," he whispered, his voice thick with tears. "So sorry."

She stirred, moaning pitifully, and Troy pressed his lips against her forehead again. "Shhh," he soothed, stroking a wide hand over her hair and along her cheek. "Everything's going to be okay now. I'm here."

Her eyelashes fluttered, then opened a slit. "Troy?"

"Yeah, sweetheart, it's me."

Her fingers tightened around his. "The baby...?"

Wanting to reassure her, he splayed a hand over her stomach, molding its shape. "He's going to be fine. Just fine."

Her fingers relaxed around his and her eyelids shuttered closed, a tear leaking from between her thick lashes to trail down her face. "I was so scared," she whispered, her lips trembling. "So scared."

Troy swept the tear away with his thumb, while trying to stem his own. "I know, sweetheart."

"Troy?"

"Yeah?"

"Hold me."

He hesitated only a second before raising a hip to the side of the bed and easing down beside her. Lifting her head from the pillow, he slid one arm beneath her shoulders and the other around her waist, curling his body protectively around hers.

She snuggled close. "You'll stay with me, won't you?"

He laid his head next to hers on the pillow. "I'm not going anywhere. Now sleep," he whispered, and pressed his lips against her forehead again. "Sleep."

Ten

———

Troy awakened to find Shelby awake, too, and staring at him. Drawing away slightly, he searched her face, looking for signs of pain or discomfort. What he found instead made his mouth go dry. Her eyes were emotionless, her expression blank. "Are you okay?" he asked hesitantly. "In pain?"

She shook her head slowly. "No. I'm fine."

"Can I get you anything? Water? Do you need help going to the rest room?"

She closed her eyes and shook her head again, then opened them to look at him with that same blank intensity. "Did my parents call you? Is that why you came?"

Reminded that they hadn't, he set his jaw, making a mental note to discuss that omission with her preacher-daddy later. "No. I found your note last night when I came in from the barn." Guilt flooded him as he remembered the words she'd penned. He laid a hand against her cheek, stroking a thumb beneath her eye. "I'm sorry, Shelby. I shouldn't have left you alone like that."

She drew away from his touch and his hand dropped to lie on the pillow between them. Fear gripped his chest as he stared at her, feeling the sting of her rejection and wondering what it meant.

"No. You did what you had to do. What you felt compelled to do."

The lifelessness in her eyes, in her voice, chilled him to the bone. "But I never meant to hurt you," he hastened to tell her. "I'd never do anything to purposefully hurt you."

A soft smile of regret touched the corners of her mouth. "No. I know you wouldn't. But you did, Troy. You hurt me really badly."

He lifted his hand to lay it against her cheek again, but she turned her face away, refusing his touch. "Shelby. Please," he whispered, fearing his heart was breaking. "I know I shouldn't have said the things I did. I was wrong. About a lot of things. I found my mother's Death Certificate. You left that for me, didn't you?"

"Yes," she said, and dipped her chin, avoiding his gaze. "I found it in the Bible. I know it was presumptuous of me to even open it, but I wanted to know more about your family. I thought perhaps I'd find the answers there."

"And you did. More than I even knew."

Her forehead creased in puzzlement as she lifted her face to look at him. "You had never seen the document?"

"No. Never." He lifted a shoulder when her expression turned doubtful. "It's Granny's Bible. I used to sit in her lap when I was a kid and look at the pictures. But I never opened it on my own. She used it like a scrapbook, filling it with bits of memories." He shrugged again self-consciously. "Sort of like a diary, I guess. Private. I never felt I was supposed to look at it uninvited."

Seeing the guilt stain her cheeks, he added quickly, "But

I don't want you to feel bad about looking in her Bible. She wouldn't mind, I'm sure. In fact, I know she wouldn't.'' He bit back a groan, knowing by her pained expression that nothing he could say would erase her guilt for prying. ''She told me that you came by the home to see her yesterday.''

''She did?''

''Yeah. She called me last night. Just before I found your note.'' He chuckled softly, remembering the conversation. ''Said I ought to slap my brand on you. That you're a keeper.'' He looked at her then, his smile melting as he met her blue gaze. Desperate to make her understand how much he loved her, how much he needed her, he took her hand, praying that he wasn't too late, that he hadn't killed whatever feelings she might have had for him. When she tried to pull away, he tightened his grip. ''Shelby—''

But the door to her room opened before he could tell her what was in his heart, about the gift she'd given him— them both, he hoped—by sharing with him the true circumstances behind his mother's death. Knowledge that had freed him of his guilt over her death.

They both turned to look toward the door where the morning duty nurse stood in the doorway, her mouth pursed in disapproval.

''Excuse me, sir,'' the nurse said pointedly. ''But the hospital beds are for our patients, not their guests.''

Troy released Shelby's hand and rolled from the bed and to his feet, combing his wild hair into place with self-conscious fingers. ''Sorry, ma'am.''

The nurse stepped to the side, holding the door open. ''I need to see to my patient's needs. If you'll excuse us,'' she added pushing the door wider, indicating that his presence wasn't needed or wanted.

Troy glanced at Shelby, hoping she'd insist that he remain. When she didn't, when she kept her face turned away from his, he dragged his hat from the bedside table. "I'll just grab me a cup of coffee in the cafeteria." He leaned to drop a kiss on Shelby's cheek before she could dodge him…and nearly crumpled when she turned her face away to stare out the window. Fearing that he'd lost whatever chance of happiness he might have had with her, he backed slowly from the bed. "I'll be back," he said, unsure whether Shelby would consider his words a threat or a promise.

Three cups of coffee later Troy decided that the nurse had had enough time to do whatever she'd needed to do, and he headed back for Shelby's room, determined to wipe away any doubts Shelby might have about him and his feelings for her. At her door he stopped, hearing voices inside.

"You're going home with your mother and me," he heard her father say, "and I won't listen to another word about it."

"But, Daddy—"

"Not another word," the preacher warned, his stern voice brooking no argument. "I should have had the marriage annulled the moment I learned of it. I knew that man wouldn't take proper care of you. Cowboys are, at their best, nothing but glorified gypsies. Living a hand-to-mouth existence, their entire lives focused on the next rodeo, never thinking of their responsibilities or their duties to their wives and families."

"Daddy!"

Troy heard the anger in Shelby's voice, the frustration. But it was nothing compared to the rage that boiled inside him. He flattened a palm against the door and shoved it open. The preacher whirled, startled by the sound of the door slamming back against the room's interior wall, then frowned when his gaze met Troy's.

Dismissing Troy with a scathing look, the preacher turned to his wife. "Pack her things. We're taking Shelby home with us."

"Like hell you are," Troy said, taking another step into the room. "*I'm* taking Shelby home. To *our* home."

The preacher spun, his face mottled with rage. "You mean to *her* apartment, don't you?"

"Her apartment or our ranch. Whichever suits her."

The preacher snorted. "And isn't that just like a cowboy? Riding in when the damage is done, the crisis is over, acting like some big-shot hero. Where were you when she needed you?" he asked, stabbing an accusing finger at Troy's chest. "When she was lying on that floor, alone and in pain? If not for her mother and me, she might have lost the baby and bled to death in that apartment."

Though the guilt bit deep, Troy refused to let it show that the preacher had hit a nerve. "I'm here now," he said, his voice rough with barely contained fury.

The preacher snorted. "A little late, I'd say. But perhaps it's best that Shelby was able to see what her future held for her if she remained married to you." He turned and extended a hand to Shelby, who sat on the side of the bed, her face pale, her lips trembling. "Come along, Shelby. We're taking you home where we can look after you and *his* baby."

Shelby fisted her hands on her lap, refusing to take her father's hand. "The baby isn't Troy's."

"What!"

Troy took another step into the room, this one longer and distance eating, quickly placing himself between Shelby and her father. Turning his back to Shelby, he braced his hands on his hips as if to shield her from her father. "Don't listen to her, Reverend. She's out of her head. Probably the trauma. Maybe the drugs."

"Now listen here," the preacher sputtered indignantly. "If that baby's not yours—"

"No, you listen," Troy said, shoving his face into the preacher's. "That's my wife and that's my baby she's carrying, and I'll be damned if I'll just sit by and let you fill her mind with lies about me and try to squeeze me out of her life. I love her, and I love that baby she's carrying, and by God *I'm* going to take care of them both, not you."

"Daniel."

The preacher tore his gaze from Troy's to look at his wife. She took him by the arm and gave him a gentle tug toward the door. "Wh-what?" he stammered, struggling against the firm grip she had on him.

"I think we should go home, dear," she said gently, continuing to propel him toward the door. "Troy's here now, and it's his place as Shelby's husband to take care of her."

The preacher glanced back, straining to peer around Troy to get a look at his daughter. "But—"

"I'm okay, Daddy," Shelby said quietly. "Really."

Marian gave her husband a gentle shove into the hallway, then caught the door and glanced back, shooting Troy a conspiratorial wink before closing it behind her.

With the preacher gone, silence seemed to hum in the room. Troy inhaled deeply, afraid to face Shelby, not at all sure if his rough treatment of her father had weakened whatever chances he might have had with her.

"Troy?"

The tears in her voice had him turning. She sat on the side of the bed, looking up at him, her eyes wide and brimming.

He dropped to a knee at her feet and took her hand in his. "What?" he asked, squeezing her fingers in his.

"You told Daddy the baby was yours."

He gulped, swallowing hard, trying to choke back the fear. "I know it was a lie, but I honestly feel as if it is."

"And you said you loved the baby."

He dipped his face over her lap, pressing his lips against their joined hands, then laid his cheek against them. "I do, Shelby. With all my heart."

He felt the weight of her hand against the side of his head, the tremble of her fingers as she combed her fingers through his hair. "I love you, Troy," she said softly, "but I don't want you here if what you feel for my baby and me is nothing but responsibility."

He lifted his head to look at her, unable to believe that she'd think such a thing. "Responsibility?"

"Yes." When he would've denied her claim, she pressed a finger against his lips, silencing him. "You're a good man, Troy. An honorable one. If nothing else, I've learned that about you over the past few weeks. You've spent your life protecting those too weak to protect themselves. But I'm not weak."

She smiled, then sniffed. "Though I used to be," she admitted sheepishly. "But you've made me realize that I am strong. The strength was there all along buried deep inside me, just waiting to burst out and strut its stuff." She laughed softly at his surprised expression, then squeezed the hand that still gripped hers. "I know now that I can take care of myself and my baby and that I can deal with whatever gossip that might arise concerning the circumstances surrounding his conception." She laid a hand against Troy's cheek, her eyes filled with tenderness as she looked deeply into his. "You don't have to take care of me any longer or protect my baby. I can do that myself."

Slowly Troy rose, drawing Shelby to her feet, as well. "I know you can," he said, his voice gruff with emotion. "I always did." He caught her other hand and squeezed both between his. "But that doesn't change how I feel about you. About the baby. I love you, Shelby. And the baby.''

"Troy," she began patiently.

He squeezed her hands, silencing her. "No. Hear me out. Please. I know that I was wrong to refuse your love when you offered it, not to accept the comfort you wanted to give me. But I honestly thought I didn't deserve your love, or you, either, for that matter. That I was tainted somehow. Marked for life for what I had done."

"Oh, Troy," she murmured softly, tears filling her eyes again.

"I lived with the guilt a long time, Shelby, thinking that I was responsible for my mother's death. You don't know what that kind of thinking can do to a person. But it never took away from the love I felt for you. I just wanted to protect you from it. From my past. From me."

Before he could say more, she tugged her hands free from his, and threw her arms around his neck. "Oh, Troy. I love you so much."

The feel of her body pressed against his, the desperation with which she clung to him, told Troy more than any words she might say. He squeezed her to him, burying his face in her hair. "Marry me, Shelby. Be my wife."

Laughing, she backed from his arms, wiping the tears from her eyes. "But we are married! Twice, in fact."

He hooked his arms around her waist and drew her to him, grinning, his heart near bursting with his love for her. "Yeah. But those two times don't count. I want us to marry again. This time for the right reasons."

Framing his face with her hands, Shelby drew him close. "You name the place and the time, and I'll be there."

He nuzzled her nose with his. "Think your daddy would do the honors again?"

Shelby drew back to look at him in surprise. "You'd

want him to perform the ceremony after the way he's treated you?''

He shrugged, then grinned. ''He's not so bad. Just a little overprotective where his daughter is concerned.''

Laughing, Shelby threw her arms around his neck. ''It's no wonder I love you. You're a good man, Troy Jacobs. The best.''

*   *   *   *   *

*Don't miss Clayton and Rena's
romance when Peggy Moreland's
exciting miniseries,*

TEXAS GROOMS

continues next month with

SLOW WALTZ ACROSS TEXAS,

*available from Silhouette Desire!
Here's a sneak preview....*

One

With dawn less than an hour away and his in-laws' estate still draped in darkness, Clayton stole across the rear lawn, keeping to the shadows and avoiding the bright patches of moonlight scattered about. Grateful that his in-laws didn't have any dogs to alert them of his approach, he reached the portico that arched between the Palmers' four-car garage and their home, and paused to study the stone column support nearest him, wondering if he could pull this off.

Knowing that a desperate situation required desperate measures, he toed off his boots and tossed his hat on top of them. Then with a resigned sigh, he planted a foot against an uneven stone and hauled himself up the side of the house and onto the roof. Breathing heavily, he stood, dusting off his clothes as he looked around.

When he found his wife's bedroom window open as he'd hoped, he eased it higher, swung a leg over the sill and ducked inside.

His heart squeezed a bit as he gazed down at his sleeping wife. Bathed in moonlight that spilled through the open window behind him, she lay on her side, one hand tucked between her cheek and her pillow.

With his gaze on her sleeping profile, he lifted a foot and dragged off first one sock, then the other. Tossing them aside, he unbuckled his belt and quickly stripped off his jeans. As he eased closer to the side of the bed, he shrugged his shirt off, then lifted the corner of the sheet and slipped beneath the covers.

Stretching out beside his wife, he propped himself up on an elbow, content, for the moment, just to watch her sleep. When the urge to touch her became too strong, he lifted a hand and stroked the tips of his fingers beneath her eyelashes, then down along her jaw.

At his fingers' soft trailing, she snuggled deeper into her pillow, her lips parting on a thready sigh. The pleasure-filled sound hummed through Clayton, calling to something deep in his soul. Unable to resist any longer, he lowered his face over hers. With a tenderness intended to seduce, he swept his tongue across her lower lip, then pressed his mouth lightly against the moisture he'd left there, warming her lips with his breath before he began to slowly sip at the sweetness beyond.

He felt another sigh vibrate against his lips, and grew still when she shifted and drew her hand languidly from beneath her cheek to loop it loosely around his neck.

From experience, Clayton knew that her response to him was unconscious, instinctive, and he knew, too, that what he was doing probably wasn't ethical, maybe not even legal…for sure not fair. But at this point he wasn't concerned about playing by any set of rules, established or not. He needed to somehow break through Rena's resistance, reestablish their relationship, remind her of what they'd once shared.

And the bedroom was the one place where they'd never had a problem communicating.

The idea to seduce his wife had come to him while he'd been lying in his bed at the hotel, alone, miserable. Scared spitless that he was going to lose his wife and family, and frustrated because he hadn't been able to get Rena alone long enough to talk to her, he had come up with this plan.

He slid his hand down the smooth column of her throat. Feeling the thrum of her pulse beneath his palm, he marveled at it a moment before he covered a breast with his hand. He stroked a thumb over her nipple, bringing it to life beneath her nightgown's thin fabric, then smoothed his palm farther down her front and to her knees, where the hem of her nightgown was bunched. Pleased to at last meet bare skin, he shaped his hand around a shapely calf and squeezed. She mewled at the gentle pressure, and he froze, holding his breath, as she shifted closer to him and molded her body against his. With her eyes still closed, she lifted her head in a blind search for his mouth. Finding it, she purred her pleasure as she curled her fingers around his neck and drew him down with her.

"Rena?" he whispered.

She hummed a lazy response against his lips, then opened her mouth to mate her tongue with his in a slow, sensual dance.

Desire stabbed through Clayton and he fought it back, determined to keep his need for her under control. Slowly, carefully, he eased her to her back. "Rena," he said again, more urgent this time.

She blinked open her eyes and slowly brought his face into focus. "Clayton?" she murmured in confusion, her voice still rough with sleep. Frowning slightly, she tried to sit up.

He pressed his mouth against hers, forcing her head back to the pillow. "Yeah, baby, it's me," he murmured. He returned his hand to her calf and dragged his knuckles slowly up her leg, easing her nightgown higher. "It's been a long time, Rena," he whispered huskily. "A damn long time." When his hand reached the juncture of her thighs, he drew back to meet her gaze. "Make love with me, Rena," he said softly.

Rena stared up at Clayton, fully awake now, her blood flowing like liquid fire through her veins. She saw the need in his eyes, the same need she knew must be mirrored in her own...and wondered if she could be dreaming. Needing the reassurance that he wasn't a figment of her imagination, a major player in a lustful dream, she laid a palm against his cheek. And nearly wept when her palm met the warmth of his flesh.

"Let me love you, Rena," he whispered.

Tears filled her eyes as she stared at him, lost in the depths of his blue eyes. She was prepared to tell him no, that it had been *too* long, and order him from her bed. But when she saw the warmth, the hope, the tenderness in his gaze, the doors of her heart flew open again, letting him in. "Yes," she whispered, gulping back tears. "Love me, Clayton."

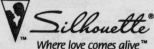

***Don't miss
an exciting opportunity
to save on the purchase of
Harlequin and Silhouette books!***

Buy any two Harlequin or
Silhouette books and save
$10.00 off future Harlequin
and Silhouette purchases

OR

buy any three
Harlequin or Silhouette books
and save **$20.00 off** future
Harlequin and Silhouette purchases.

***Watch for details
coming in October 2000!***

PHQ400

If you enjoyed what you just read,
then we've got an offer you can't resist!

Take 2 bestselling love stories FREE!

Plus get a FREE surprise gift!

COMING NEXT MONTH

#1315 SLOW WALTZ ACROSS TEXAS—Peggy Moreland
Man of the Month/Texas Grooms
Growing up an orphan had convinced cowboy Clayton Rankin that he didn't need anyone. But when his wife, Rena, told him he was about to lose her, he was determined to win back her love—and have his wife teach him about matters of the heart!

#1316 ROCK SOLID—Jennifer Greene
Body & Soul
She needed to unwind. But when Lexie Woolf saw Cash McKay, relaxation was the last thing on her mind. Cash was everything Lexie had dreamed of in a man—except she feared *she* was not the woman for *him.* Could Cash convince Lexie that their love was rock solid?

#1317 THE NEXT SANTINI BRIDE—Maureen Child
Bachelor Battalion
They were supposed to be together for only one night of passion, but First Sergeant Dan Mahoney couldn't forget Angela Santini. So he set out to seduce the single mom—one tantalizing touch at a time—and convince her that all her nights were meant to be spent with him!

#1318 MAIL-ORDER CINDERELLA—Kathryn Jensen
Fortune's Children: The Grooms
Tyler Fortune needed a bride—and plain librarian Julie Parker fit the bill. But Tyler never counted on falling for his convenient wife. Now he needed to convince Julie that she was the perfect mate for him—so he could become her husband in every way.

#1319 LADY WITH A PAST—Ryanne Corey
She thought no one knew of her former notoriety, but when Connor Garrett tracked down Maxie Calhoon, she had to face her past. Connor stirred emotions in Maxie that she had never experienced, but did he love the woman she once was or the one she had become?

#1320 DOCTOR FOR KEEPS—Kristi Gold
The last thing Dr. Rick Jansen needed was to fall for his new nurse, Miranda Brooks. Yet there was something about Miranda that made it impossible to keep his thoughts—and hands—away from her. But would he still desire Miranda when he learned her secret?

CMN0800